THE
CORVETTE
MYSTERY

THE
CORVETTE
MYSTERY

For Cindy,
Enjoy
Eric Johnson

E R I C   J O H N S O N

TATE PUBLISHING
AND ENTERPRISES, LLC

Published by Tate Publishing & Enterprises, LLC
127 E. Trade Center Terrace | Mustang, Oklahoma 73064 USA
1.888.361.9473 | www.tatepublishing.com

Tate Publishing is committed to excellence in the publishing industry. The company reflects the philosophy established by the founders, based on Psalm 68:11,
"The Lord gave the word and great was the company of those who published it."

Book design copyright © 2014 by Tate Publishing, LLC. All rights reserved.
Cover design by Junriel Boquecosa
Interior design by Honeylette Pino

Published in the United States of America

ISBN: 978-1-62854-124-3
Fiction / Mystery & Detective / General
14.01.22

CHAPTER 1

Since he had entered an all-Corvette car show, Roger Strong thought of his fellow exhibitors not so much as competitors as they were colleagues with a love for the same kind of car. He was aware that not all of the Corvette owners thought the same way. There were colorful, highly-polished Corvettes as far in every direction as he could see—the entire south two-thirds of the lot of Jerry's Chevrolet. Banners and flags were flapping in the breeze under the warm sun. He loved these shows.

Roger had entered his 2004 Millennium Yellow Corvette convertible. There were two broad classifications of cars in the show—stock and modified. Since he was an unrepentant hot rodder, he had modified his Corvette in a number of ways. He had started by replacing the original engine with a far more powerful engine from a Z06 Corvette. When asked why he didn't simply buy a Z06, he replied that it was not available as a convertible, and he had to drive a convertible Corvette. When the engine swap was completed, he added massive amounts of chrome under the hood and installed a black leather custom interior.

After he had finished dusting his car and was about to polish it with detail spray, he stood a moment thinking that it felt very warm for the month of May in South Dakota. He heard his name called.

"Dr. Strong. Dr. Strong."

Emily Flowers greatly preferred being called "Em'ly"—as was common in the

Midwest. She was walking slowly across the pavement from the stock Corvette section. She was showing an extremely rare copper-colored 1955 Corvette that she had inherited when her brother was killed. She had been one of Roger's most talented students at the university a few years earlier. Because of her playful interest in the English language, he had told her that she would enjoy being an English major, but she loved art too much to switch majors. Her family was quite wealthy, and she didn't need to consider which major would lead to a better job.

"Do you like my new show outfit?" Em'ly turned her head, shook her short pixie hair cut, and struck a mock pose like a runway model. As was customary for an art major, Em'ly had posed for some undergraduate drawing classes, and she could have been a professional model. Her metallic copper tank top complemented her orange slacks. She broke the pose with an embarrassed laugh.

"I used to wear these slacks when I showed my tangerine bam slammed PT Cruiser, and yesterday I found this top at the mall and it looks perfect with my new car."

"Since you're exhibiting a stock Corvette, you're not permitted to modify the car, but there's no rule about modifying your clothing." He smiled.

"I don't know about the clothing, but you're sure right about the Corvette. The judges check every hose clamp and nut and bolt. They even crawl under the car to look at the frame and mufflers. This isn't an official National Corvette Restorers Society event, but the judges seem to apply the NCRS standards for stock Corvettes." She quoted an NCRS manual in a solemn official voice: "The cars must appear and function exactly as they did when they left the factory."

Roger nodded. He knew something about the NCRS standards, and he had a begrudging respect for them. "Some day I would like to show a first-generation Corvette, a 1953 to 1962, and, of course, then I would religiously follow the NCRS regulations."

"I like your mellow yellow car—you've modified exactly the right things."

"Thanks, Em'ly."

The look on her face became serious and solemn. "Dr. Strong, can I ask you something?" Roger motioned toward the chairs behind his car, and both of them sat down. The exhibitor next to them was frantically polishing the hood of his car and was not near enough to overhear their conversation.

Em'ly was silent a moment. "As I show this Corvette, I'm reminded that it was restored by my brother Gordy, and he'd still be showing it if he had not been murdered. His killer hasn't been found."

"No doubt the police are doing all that they can." Roger spoke reluctantly because he knew it sounded like a feeble excuse.

"I suppose they are. But could you help? You assisted the sheriff in the Jarndyce mystery. Could you do the same thing for Gordy?"

"Well, in the Jarndyce case, cars were involved, and I gave the sheriff the benefit of my experience working on cars and showing them."

"The same thing might be true with Gordy. He might have been killed because of his car. His 1955 Corvette is totally rare— only about 700 Corvettes were built in that year, and only 15 were copper color. The car has been restored to be absolutely perfect. When it's entered in a show, no other stock Corvette seems to have a chance of winning. I think Gordy's murderer was a jealous Corvette owner."

Roger was rather taken back. This was a serious charge to bring against one of their fellow Corvette exhibitors. He was quiet for several minutes. When he spoke, he continued Em'ly's train of thought. "The 1955 is the first year of the famous small-block Chevy V-8, and it's the lightest Corvette ever made. And, yes, this car has been restored perfectly. Its fit and finish inside and out are flawless. I can understand why it always wins trophies and, of course, that would be resented by those who exhibit other Corvettes."

"Poor Gordy was simply jogging out by the airport, and I think he was killed by one of these Corvette guys who competed in shows against him. I'm sure of it. Will you talk to the sheriff? You know him."

"He's a friend. The Sheriff's Department is the appropriate law enforcement unit to do the investigation. And, yes, I can have a chat with him."

"I'd better get back to my car. I left my younger brother, Ben, looking after it, but Ben's not a car guy like Gordy was, and I don't like leaving it too long." She popped up from her chair, took a few steps, and turned back. "Thank you. And your chrome engine looks great with the yellow paint—it makes me faint."

Roger stood and slowly walked up to his car. He finished polishing his Corvette with synthetic detailing spray and misted the highly polished stainless-steel parts under the hood with glass cleaner and polished them. He pulled on gloves and applied dressing on the tires—being careful not to miss a spot but using no more dressing than necessary. He threw away the gloves and put on another pair, and he put a few drops of leather conditioner on a cloth and went over the seats and most of the interior. He threw away those gloves and sprayed glass cleaner on the windshield and wiped and polished it with heavy-duty paper towels. He stepped back and looked over his car, made a dive to remove a smudge, and stood back again. It looked good. He put the sprays and dusters back in one of his show bags and sat down again.

Next to Roger's car, a 1953 Commemorative Edition Corvette was parked. It was a modern Corvette, it had an engine, transmission, and running gear similar to those in Roger's car, but the body panels and interior had been replaced with stylized parts that resembled those of a 1953 Corvette. The car was greatly admired by almost every spectator, but it didn't win many trophies—probably because the car's owner neglected to thoroughly clean the car—although he took great pains to polish the most visible portions—the hood, tops of the fenders, and trunk lid.

The owner of the Commemorative Edition was the president of Roger's bank. He continued to furiously polish the hood of his car. He was certainly intent on what he was doing—he had not even looked up when he exchanged a greeting with Roger. By contrast, the spectators who drifted by were very friendly and outgoing—they almost always were awed by Roger's completely polished engine.

Two judges with clipboards approached. One of them was a trainee judge—in introducing himself he said, "I'm Brayden, and I'm green behind the ears." They looked closely at the paint, staring down the lines of the car from the front and from the back. They examined the interior by leaning into the convertible and by asking Roger to open both doors. They seemed to be very careful not to touch the car.

When Brayden saw the massive and unusual amount of polished stainless steel under the hood, he said, "Wow! You sure have set your own chart." Both judges seemed fascinated by the after-market exhaust system and the fact that Roger had polished the four stainless steel tips both outside and inside as far as the eye could see.

"Great attention to detail," the senior judge said.

Brayden nodded in agreement. "You hit it in a nutshell."

They looked intently at the oversize tires and the large highly-polished aluminum wheels. They moved closer and peered past the wheel spokes at the disk brakes. Roger had coated the brake calipers with special yellow paint to match the color of his car.

Roger and the judges looked up to see two additional Corvettes entering the show area. "More water over the bridge," Brayden said. He thought a moment and added, "Perhaps I mean that it's more water under the dam." The two judges stood up and wrote on their clipboards and added up Roger's score. As they walked away, the senior judge showed his total to Brayden, and he nodded and said, "He should like that score. Or, as they say, he should put that in his tailpipe and smoke it."

A man named Jerry Ford owned Jerry's Chevrolet. When he had the opportunity to acquire the dealership, he thought it would be a scream to advertise, "Jerry Ford Chevrolet." People wouldn't know what brand of car was being sold. However, his ad agency advised him to call it simply "Jerry's Chevrolet," and that's what he reluctantly did. He enjoyed sponsoring car shows, and he liked walking around among the cars and greeting the exhibitors.

"Hi, Roger." He laughed, and he leaned forward and rocked back and forth. "Your car sure looks great. This Millennium Yellow paint, GM code #79, is very hot. And speaking of things that are hot (and he laughed again), I still remember that chili that you made for us!"

Jerry had been part of a group that Roger had invited for a chili dinner. Roger often got carried away when he was cooking, and on that occasion he had put far too many peppers in the chili. His guests were polite and ate at least part of the contents of the bowl put in front of them, but they were not very comfortable for hours afterward.

Jerry continued laughing and nodding as he moved toward the next Corvette. Its owner continued compulsively polishing his car, but he looked up wondering what the joke was. Roger resumed watching the spectators. Occasionally someone would stop and ask a question about the car, and Roger was always happy to talk about his Corvette and probably supplied far more information than was wanted.

At 5:00 p.m., Jerry took the microphone to announce the winners in the competition. He first laughed jovially, bowed from the waist, and laughed again. As he rocked back and forth, he awarded thirty-seven trophies: first, second, and third place trophies for all six generations of Corvettes—for both stock and modified classes—plus another for Best in Show. For her C1, Em'ly won first place. Roger won first place for his modified C5.

The compulsive polisher who was parked next to Roger won the trophy for his modified C1. It was not a surprise to those who appreciated Corvettes that Em'ly's 1955 Corvette also won the Best in Show trophy.

Roger put his trophy on the passenger seat and his show bag on the floor of his car. He put the top up so that he could start the air conditioning. He drove forward toward the street with a smooth motion. He had formerly shown street rods, and they always started with a lurch and the ride was harsh, and they certainly did not have air conditioning. At the end of a long day in the hot sun, he had a much more comfortable ride home after a show in his Corvette than in a hot rod.

Inching toward the main exit, he seemed to be in the slowest-moving line of Corvettes. Some of the drivers ahead of him snorted their loud exhaust with impatience as they waited. Roger felt a wave of anger at the delay. He smiled and waved to Em'ly and Ben Flowers as they passed him in another line, and he turned his thoughts to what he would say to the sheriff about the murder of their brother.

CHAPTER 2

Professor Roger Strong finished teaching his last afternoon class, and he walked home with a bundle of papers under his arm that he would read that night. He enjoyed the short walk in the bright spring sun. He was a former football player, and he liked almost any kind of exercise. He was in good physical shape, although he was a little more bulky than he should be because, as he reflected, he did not get enough exercise. As he thought about his bulky physique, he remembered that he had not had any lunch, and he was hungry.

He was removing his tie as he opened the back door of his large Victorian home two blocks from campus. He walked through his large kitchen and put the papers on a chair in his study and changed into the jeans and T-shirt that he wore to work on his cars. He noticed that the clean T-shirt had a black grease stain on the front that had not been removed in the wash, but he didn't care.

He returned to his spacious kitchen and stood considering what he would make to eat. Living alone as he did, Roger could cook what he liked at any time he liked. He wanted a Maid-Rite sandwich.

As a kid, Roger had gone to a gleaming stainless steel diner that sold only one kind of sandwich or burger. They were called Maid-Rite sandwiches, and he had enjoyed eating them. He had not seen or tasted a Maid-Rite for decades, and then one day as he was attempting to make something called a crunch burger, he discovered that it tasted something like a Maid-Rite. He modified the recipe until it tasted exactly like the Maid-Rite that he remembered and loved. That's what he wanted for his late lunch.

He made a white sauce. First he melted several tablespoons of butter over low heat in a heavy saucepan. He slowly added an equal number of tablespoons of flour and blended the flour with the melted butter. He added salt and pepper. He slowly stirred in two cups of milk. As the mixture cooked, he added three or four cloves, continued stirring, and then removed the cloves—he wanted just a hint of clove taste.

Meanwhile he browned two pounds of ground beef in a separate pan. As the beef cooked, he added a diced white onion, salt, pepper, and powdered oregano. He diced ten medium mushrooms, and pureed them. When the beef was brown, he drained the liquid, and added the pureed mushrooms and the white sauce. He stirred the mixture and covered it and let it simmer over very low heat.

When he tasted his concoction fifteen minutes later, it was almost perfect. He added a little more oregano and let it simmer a little longer. When he tasted it again, it was perfect. He put a package of hamburger buns on the table and opened a bag of potato chips. He sat at his table and made and ate one Maid-Rite sandwich after another. They were excellent.

When he felt stuffed, he pushed back from the table. Roger knew that his lunch had about a million calories. While he remained fit in his early thirties, he knew he should watch his weight. Oh well, he would simply skip eating any supper. He headed for his garage to replace the tail lamps in his Corvette with brighter LED bulbs.

Sheriff Joseph Bucket was known as a tough, hard-working law enforcement officer. His friends always called him "Joey." When he was done with his official duties for the day, the tall, lanky policeman frequently dropped in to visit Roger as he worked in his garage.

The two men had gotten to be friends after the sheriff had been forced to arrest Roger. At a car show, a spectator who was a former football teammate of Roger's had made boorish, insulting remarks about one of his friends—Em'ly Flowers. Roger had always disliked this guy, and he had told him to shut up. When the teammate had walked over and pushed him, Roger had pushed back, and both had exchanged punches, and by the time the sheriff arrived, the two were on the ground and Roger was on top and would not stop pounding him—even when the sheriff had ordered him to stop. Roger had to be pulled off, and he was taken to jail where he spent the night. The next morning, a judge had ruled that he must attend anger management classes. Later, Roger had thanked the sheriff for restraining him, he knew that his anger was a problem, and he thought he now could keep it under control.

Roger looked up from his work on his tail lamps to see the tall frame of the sheriff at the door. "Dr. Strong, if you don't give me a cold beer immediately, I will collapse. In fact, I'm going to collapse anyway." He threw himself down on a beat-up leather couch.

"Bad day, Joey?" Roger asked the reclining police officer as he took a bottle of beer from the refrigerator and handed it to him.

"Yes. Early this morning, a team from the State Office of Public Safety descended on us, and they left only a few minutes ago. They inspected all of our equipment and criticized everything we did. They didn't like our guns, and our training of new deputies is deeply flawed." He pronounced "deeply flawed" in a phony falsetto voice.

"What's wrong with your guns?"

"They said our .40 caliber pistols were too powerful for use on the street. We switched to them because the FBI recommended them for police departments, and we like them and they are effective. The team wants us to go back to the old .38 special."

"And your training of new officers?"

"Oh, that's all wrong too! We should train them to shoot by holding the pistol in one hand—rather than with both hands. Ha! If one hand is better than two, perhaps holding the pistol with two fingers would be better yet!"

Roger laughed and said, "Settle down and drink your beer." He finished replacing the bulbs in the taillights of his Corvette. He turned on the lights and walked back to look at them; the LED bulbs were much brighter than the original equipment. Looking pleased, he shut off the car's lights and then took a beer from the refrigerator for himself.

Roger's garage was the friendliest room in his house. The over-stuffed couch and easy chair had seen better days, and the leather was scuffed and worn, but they were soft and comfortable. The floor had black-and-white checkered tile that reflected the bright halogen lights. The sweet scents of car polish, detail spray, and leather dressing hung in the air. It was cozy and snug.

Roger sat on a stool by his workbench. "I have a question to ask you about something else, but do you want to whine a little more first?"

"I want to whine. That state team is composed of pencil pushers who have never shot a gun in the line of duty—maybe never shot a gun at all. I don't know why those pinheads are sent out here!" Joey was silent for a moment. "Okay. I'm done for now."

Roger couldn't help smiling at the sheriff's frustration, but he wanted to discuss a serious topic. "I saw Em'ly Flowers at the Corvette show this weekend. She thinks that her brother Gordy was killed by someone who was envious of her brother's Corvette and the trophies it won. She asked me to talk with you."

Joey's attention was immediately captured, and he sat up. "Is it likely that an envious car guy killed Gordy Flowers?"

"She's convinced of it. I suppose it *is* possible. I don't know much about the killing. Can you tell me what happened?"

"There isn't a lot to tell. Em'ly's brother was the founder, owner, and CEO of Gordon Flowers Investments, Inc. He was very successful. The family has money, and he was making a lot more. He worked long days, and rarely took off a day. He had a standard routine for his time immediately after work— he left his business at 6:00 p.m., drove to his townhouse and changed clothes, jogged on the same route down his street to the cemetery near the airport and jogged back, showered, and had dinner.

"About six months ago, he left his house for his jog and didn't return. An airport mechanic returning to work on a plane at 8:00 p.m. found his body on the side of the road near a hanger. He had been shot three times. Another airport employee reported seeing a man walking in the area, and shortly after that man left, a woman was seen. He didn't recognize either the man or woman."

"What evidence did you collect?"

"Not much. The coroner recovered three .22 caliber slugs from the body. There were no powder burns on the body, so the shooter was not real close to him, and the shots are spaced from near the neck to the waist, which would indicate that they were made from a distance, although perhaps the shooter was simply a pretty bad shot. The time of death could have been as much as an hour before the body was found. We pressed the airport employee to describe the man and woman he had seen, but he said that he had simply glanced at them, and he could say only that the man wore a green shirt and the woman had on a pink coat."

"Who had a reason to kill Gordy?"

"I thought a lot about motive. I wondered who would benefit from his death. When Gordy's estate was settled, his younger brother, Ben, inherited the business and half of his fortune, and his little sister, Em'ly, inherited the other half plus a 1955 Corvette. That was appropriate since Ben had said that he was interested in the business, although his friends say he is more focused on partying. In any case, he has little interest in cars, and Em'ly loves cars and is active in showing them. The infusion of inherited money was exactly what Ben badly needed. He had been deep in debt, especially due to the lavish house he had built by the lake. And he's always hosting parties there. Although Em'ly didn't seem to be a likely offender, she loved Gordy's Corvette so much, we had to look at her too.

"About the time I thought we had two suspects, I found that both had alibis. Both Ben and Em'ly were out of state when the shooting took place. Ben was in Dallas in some kind of technical school for managers run by a computer company—it turned out that he didn't do well in the course in which he was enrolled because he was spending too much time in the Dallas clubs. Em'ly was in Chicago viewing an opening exhibit of nineteenth-century art.

"Frankly, we were at a dead end with this case, but you suggest a whole new line of investigation. How can we determine the car owners who were in competition with Gordy's Corvette?"

"The managers of recent shows would have records of entries. A comparison of the cars in several shows would indicate the people who frequently competed with Gordy."

"Can you do that?"

"I will." Roger thought a few moments. "You know that Em'ly is showing Gordy's Corvette now—is she in danger?"

"She could be. I will ask deputies to keep an eye on her."

CHAPTER 3

T he early morning sun streamed through Roger's windows as he sat at his computer checking his email. After deleting lots of spam and laughing at a message a university colleague had forwarded to him, he sent an email to the regional director of car shows, a man he knew only as Bitzer. He was a lineal descendent of a man with the same name who had been a light porter for the well-known author Charles Dickens. Both the regional director and the ancestor were very thorough, although they hurried and rushed every action. In his email, Roger asked for lists of cars and their owners for the last year of car shows in which Corvettes had been entered. Within minutes, Roger received an email from Bitzer with more than three dozen attached files.

Roger needed to correlate the cars and owners on the lists to determine which Corvettes were competing with Gordy's 1955 Corvette. He had learned to write applications in the SNOBOL programming language, and it would be ideal for his purpose. The application that Roger wrote identified the shows in which Gordy's car was entered, and it collected the names of the owners of all Corvettes in each of those shows. He found that only one person had entered a Corvette in each show that Gordy entered.

That evening, Roger called Joey and asked him to stop and help him to install something on his Corvette. The sheriff arrived a few minutes later. "So what are you doing to that yellow beast now?"

"I want to mount these three acrylic mirrors on the inside of my trunk lid. The double-sided tape supplied with the mirrors does not hold them firmly, and when the lid is slammed closed, the mirrors fall off. I was so angry, I threw the box of tape the length of the garage! I purchased some industrial strength adhesive, but it eats through the back of the mirrors and is visible from the front. I complained to the company, and I was sent another set of mirrors. I want to try this automotive trim adhesive. The problem is that the stuff takes a little while to dry, and each mirror must be held firmly in place while it's drying. That's where you come in—I need a designated holder."

"I think I can do that."

Roger carefully spread a thin, even amount of the gooey adhesive on the underside of the trunk lid, and another layer on the back of the first of the three mirrors. He pressed the mirror in place and asked Joey to hold it as he prepared the next mirror.

"I got the information that you asked for. The only Corvette that has been in every show this last year with Gordy's Corvette is owned by Darrell Yorick."

"Do you know him?"

"Yes. Slightly. I know that he is the president of the bank where I have checking and savings accounts, but my business is certainly not at a level to deal with a bank president. More significantly, I see him at shows. In fact, his Corvette was parked next to me in Jerry's recent show. He owns and shows an extremely interesting car. It is a stylized 1953 Corvette body fitted over a modern Corvette frame, engine, and running gear. Thus, it has the styling of the first year of the marque, mated to the performance, technology, and dependability of a new model."

The sheriff who had little interest in show cars looked a little irritated, as if he had been given too much irrelevant information. "Does he win lots of trophies?"

"Not nearly as many as he would like. Hard-core Corvette guys don't know what to make of his car. Sometimes they don't even know what class it should be entered in. And also, Yorick doesn't seem to notice that he is not thoroughly cleaning his car for a show. I pointed out a spot of grime on his rocker panels once, and he acted as if I had insulted him. I was trying to do him a favor. Okay, now hold this center mirror."

"How many more mirrors are going in here?"

"Only one more. Darrell Yorick is an unusual man. He seems to be a compulsive automobile detailer. He told me that he cleans and polishes his Corvette every Saturday morning—without fail—regardless of whether he would soon be showing it or whether he has even driven it since the last polish. As a bachelor, he probably has time on his hands when he's not at his job. He told me that he makes an appointment to have his oil changed late in the day when the shop is not very busy, and while the car is in the air on the hoist and the technician is draining the oil and changing the filter, Yorick cleans and polishes the underside of his car. When his car is exhibited in a show, he is a blur of polishing activity. He spends almost no time (unlike the other exhibitors) relaxing in a chair behind his car. However, one thing is odd—despite all the time and effort Yorick spends cleaning and detailing his Corvette, he misses things. I noticed that tire dressing had been slung up onto the paint behind all four wheels at the last show."

The sheriff nodded. "All I know about him is that he is the president of a bank— apparently a flourishing bank. I wonder if he had dealings with Flowers's investment business. He might have multiple reasons for wanting Gordy out of the way."

"Last mirror. I can't help you with the banking side, but from what I see of Darrell Yorick showing his car, I can testify that he would envy anyone whose Corvette won more trophies than his."

Both men stepped back and looked at the mirrors on the underside of the trunk lid. They beautifully reflected the chrome trunk lid hardware and the bright yellow carpet that Roger had installed.

"Now, the conclusive test." Roger slammed the lid. They didn't hear anything fall into the trunk. Roger gingerly opened the lid. The mirrors were firmly in place. "Ah, perfect."

As the sheriff was leaving, he said, "Thanks for the information. You have given me subjects for reflection."

"Ah, exactly like these mirrors!"

The next morning, as Roger walked toward the campus to teach his early class, he looked up at the clear sky. Rain was predicted, but it would probably hit the following day. He ran over in his mind the points that he wanted to make in the class discussion of assigned poetry by Browning and Tennyson. He felt the warm sun on his back as he climbed up the steps of his office building.

The moment Roger's class meeting was finished, he hurried back to his office, dumped his books on his desk, and rushed to the seminar room on the third floor. He was one of the four faculty members of the Promotion and Tenure Committee, and every second of the meetings of that committee was important since the future of his fellow faculty was decided.

As Roger walked into the meeting, the academic vice president, the committee chair, closed the door and called the meeting to order. "Our last meeting was a little over seven months ago, and I have distributed the minutes for it. I must remind you that the proceedings of this committee are confidential. Since the action of that last meeting was to deny tenure to Dr. Rebecca Whelk, those minutes must be unusually private and held in strict confidence."

Roger well remembered that meeting. Rebecca's dean, Dr. Keith Jefferson, had presented a very strong negative assessment of her teaching. He acknowledged that she had some impressive scholarship—especially a recent article—but he said that her students simply were not learning from her. When he observed her teaching, he carefully watched the body language of her students. Clearly her technical language about literature confused them. A student asked a question, and he was told sharply that the answer was covered in the assigned reading. There were no other questions after that. The students took few notes, and they gave each other bewildered looks and rolled their eyes. Roger argued that Rebecca should be given some kind of training or peer advising to improve her teaching, but others thought it was too late. The vote was 6-2 to deny tenure. She would be given a one-year term contract that would not be renewed.

Roger had been granted tenure as soon as he had applied for it, but he had felt more than a little anxiety about the decision. He knew that being denied tenure could mean the end of an academic career. He didn't wonder that Rebecca was bitter. He saw her stride down the hallways of his building like a wounded lioness that would attack at the slightest provocation. When she spoke to anyone, she had a sarcastic, contemptuous tone. She would badmouth her dean Dr. Jefferson, to anyone who would listen.

The faculty member being considered at the current meeting had characteristics that were the opposite of Rebecca's. He had published only a few book reviews, but he was acknowledged to be an outstanding teacher by students, faculty, and his dean. The vote was 8-0 to grant him tenure.

As Roger walked home from campus that afternoon, tenure decisions gradually faded from his mind and his thoughts turned to Corvettes. The National Corvette Restorers Society had very high standards, and they intrigued him. He wondered how difficult it would be to buy a fairly nice first-generation Corvette and restore it to a condition that would win NCRS Top Flight status. He had examined Em'ly's 1955, and he knew that most Corvettes that are for sale were far from that kind of perfect condition.

He poured over automotive sites on the internet. He looked at Corvette sites and at those that specialized in sports cars and at sites that sold all types of cars. He found hundreds of Corvettes, but only a handful of cars were what he was looking for, and the prices were outrageously high. He traveled half way across the country to look at Corvettes, and they were always disappointments. Sometimes parts were missing and often they had been in serious crashes and one car was not even the same year that it was represented to be.

One day at lunch in the faculty cafeteria, Roger was relating to a math professor how difficult it was to find a nice early Corvette. Rebecca Whelk happened to be sitting across the table from them, and she was telling a story about how she refused to go to dinner with a wealthy banker because she thought he was married, but she found out later that he was single. She thought it was a good joke. When she heard the word "Corvette," she barged into Roger's conversation. "I saw a beautiful turquoise Corvette in my hometown when I visited about six months ago. The owner was trying to sell it."

Roger was interested. "Where did you see the car?"

"I was in New Canaan, Connecticut. It's a cultured town in the heart of civilization, and you wouldn't be familiar with it. I was visiting with a classmate at a school reunion. We were talking about something else, and he remarked that he would like to sell his Corvette because it was a fragile collector car that he was afraid to drive very much."

Roger felt a flash of anger at the implication that he wouldn't be familiar with a town that was cultured and civilized. He knew that he had to keep his anger under control. He calmed himself by slowly and methodically piling pickles on his hamburger. Then he neatly squirted ketchup on the pickles. "What's your friend's name?"

At first, Rebecca looked reluctant to name her friend, but she did spit it out. "Tom Weed. He owns Weed and Duryea Hardware."

"I might try to contact him." Roger definitely wanted to know more about this Corvette.

CHAPTER 4

On a very dark morning, Roger walked quickly from his home toward the campus. It was raining. When he woke early in the dark, it had been thundering, and he had hoped he could get to his office building before the heavens opened, but not so. The rain was heavy, and the wind swirled the water around him. He buttoned his coat at the neck and put up his collar.

It was Monday, and Roger was always glad to start a new week. He had some great ideas about how he would cover the poetry of John Keats in his English literature class. As he approached his office building, he saw sheriff's cars with lights flashing—they seemed to be everywhere. Yellow police tape was stretched across the sidewalk leading to the Business School, the building next to Roger's office building. Bewildered, he stopped and stood looking at the ivy-covered building. The lights in every room in the building seemed to be turned on. People pulling on police raincoats were running up and down the front stairs. Some of them carried black cases of equipment and supplies.

Roger slowly walked toward his office building—with frequent glances toward the Business School. He walked in and shook off his wet coat and entered the office of the College of Arts and Sciences. "What in the world is going on in the Business School?"

Phyllis, the College office manager didn't immediately answer his question, but she walked over to Roger and said in a low tone, "Apparently Dean Tyler has been killed."

"What?"

"When I arrived here a little before 8:00 a.m., the junior secretary of the Business School was standing at my door. She was shaking like a leaf. She said she had noticed the light on in the dean's office when she arrived at work, and she knocked and started to say something to Dean Tyler as she pushed the door open, and she found him dead at his desk. She said there was blood all over the desk. She was terrified and ran over here, and we called 911 at once."

"Bill Tyler is dead?"

Phyllis nodded. "I think so."

"And someone killed him?"

"Well, she said there was blood all over. That doesn't sound like a natural death—does it?"

"I suppose not."

As Phyllis and Roger stood talking, Dr. Jefferson walked in the door. "What happened over in Business?"

Phyllis walked into Dr. Jefferson's office with him and started to relate the information that she knew. Roger wandered into the hallway and crossed through a dark, empty classroom and looked out the window toward the business building. He could see figures passing back and forth in the dean's office, and there was the occasional flash of a camera.

Roger shook his head as he walked up the stairs to his office. Apparently the world had become a dangerous place. First Gordy Flowers was killed, and now, a few months later, Bill Tyler was dead. He put his wet coat on a coat rack in his office and sat behind his desk and started looking at his notes for British literature, but his mind continued to wander back to what had happened in the Business building. If Bill Tyler had been murdered, who would have done such a thing? Was it a robbery? Were others in danger?

When Roger arrived home after teaching his classes, he changed into the clothes he wore to work on cars and went into his kitchen to make himself a late lunch. He cut a tomato and put the slices on a plate, and lightly salted the tomato and shook on dry leaves of oregano, and then he covered those slices with a few strands of white onion. He put the plate of tomatoes and onion in his oven to heat them, and he made toast. When the toast was brown, he put the hot tomato and onion on the toast and added slices mozzarella cheese on the top and put the toast on a pan under the broiler. When the cheese was melted, he cut the toast and put it on a plate. The simple flavors of tomato, onion, and cheese melded into a new taste that he loved.

After eating, he dialed the sheriff's office. As expected, the dispatcher told him that the sheriff was not in the building. "Please tell Sheriff Bucket that Roger could use his assistance in changing some tires and wheels. Ask him to stop when he is done for the day."

Roger had ordered a new set of Goodyear Eagle F1 GS-D3 run-flat tires for his Corvette, and they had been delivered to his garage. He had asked that instructions for the freight company be printed on the label so that the tires were not left at his front door. Space was limited on the label, but one line was added—below his name, the label read, "Roger's Garage." It made him laugh since the label made it seem as if he were operating a business, but, in any case, the tires were correctly left at the door to his garage.

Roger loved the swooshing V tread design of the new tires, and they were rated at a continuous speed of 186 miles per hour. They were mounted on chrome wheels and had been balanced (with weights only on the insides of the wheels, please). He needed simply to put them on his car in place of the current wheels and tires. He had cleaned the new tires and wheels and used chrome polish and clear coat on both sides of the wheels—it would protect the metal as well as make them shine.

About 5:30, Joey Bucket walked into the garage. The sheriff was obviously off duty since he was wearing a T-shirt and jeans. "Bucket reporting as ordered, sir!" He grinned. "How can I be of service?"

"I want to replace the wheels and tires on my Corvette, and it's easier if two people do it."

"Okay. What should we do first?"

"First, we need to jack up one side of the car. Notice that the painted fiberglass body panels wrap around the bottom of the car and they are lower than the frame. Therefore, we can't simply put a jack on the frame—the body panels would be damaged. We need to use these low-profile floor jacks after we replace the jack cradles with these lift pads."

"They look like hockey pucks."

"Indeed, some Corvette guys call them hockey pucks. Can you tell me what happened on the campus today?"

"The 911 emergency center received a frantic phone call at 7:55 this morning from a secretary in the Business College saying that the dean was dead. She talked about blood everywhere. The center dispatched an ambulance and deputies to the building, and I was there too. The EMTs were examining the body when I arrived. They called the coroner."

"Did he die this morning?"

"There is some contradictory evidence. The coroner says that he died sometime last night. The assumption is that he was shot as he worked in his office early last night. Since he is not married, no one missed him when he didn't return home. However, the bottoms of his pants were damp as if he had been walking in the morning rain.

"In any case, the secretary who arrived in the college office before 8:00 noticed that there was light under the door of his office. He might have turned it on last night or this morning—remember that it was a dark, rainy morning. She found him slumped over his desk."

"And he was shot?"

"Yes. Three times. Apparently with a .38 caliber gun."

"Okay, now notice that there are slots in the frame of the Corvette. They are called 'jacking points.' Actually, I think they were designed to be used to hold the car secure on the transport truck. Anyway, put the oblong end of the hockey puck in the frame holes and the round end on the jack."

Roger paused. "Was this a robbery gone bad?"

"It does not appear so. He still had his expensive watch, several rings, and his billfold with about one hundred dollars."

They worked in silence as they removed the plastic covers, loosened the lug nuts, jacked the wheels off the ground, and removed the wheels and tires.

"Since Tyler was shot three times, his death couldn't have been suicide," Roger said when they paused in their work.

"And no gun was found in his office."

"So somebody deliberately killed Dean Tyler. Who had a motive?"

"That is what I was going to ask you. Was a faculty member angry about something? Perhaps not receiving tenure?"

Roger thought. "I'm on the Promotion and Tenure Committee, and so I know that the faculty in the Business School who were eligible for tenure received it. In fact, only one person was denied tenure this year."

"Who was that?"

"We need to use a torque wrench on the new lug nuts. And anything that is torqued should have appropriate lubrication. Put a small dab of petroleum jelly on the threads of the axle stud before you put on the lug nut."

When both wheels were held by lightly-tightened lug nuts, the jacks were lowered and the lug nuts were torqued to 100 foot-pounds. Then the process was repeated with the two wheels on the other side of the car.

"There. The new tires look great and I have the satisfaction of knowing that these are real chrome lug nuts."

"You were going to tell me the name of the one faculty member who did not get tenure this year."

"I didn't forget your question. I was thinking about it as we worked. The actions of the Promotion and Tenure Committee are confidential. However, in this case, I think I can tell you in confidence. Tenure was denied to Rebecca Whelk."

"Is she in Tyler's college?"

"No. She is in Arts and Sciences."

"Would she have any grudge against Tyler?"

"I don't think so. At least I don't see why she would."

"So we're back where we were."

"No, we are way ahead of where we were. My new wheels and tires are mounted on my car now."

In spite of wanting to remain serious, Joey couldn't help smiling. "Give me a bottle of beer as payment for my expert assistance."

CHAPTER 5

The largest car show in the Midwest was held the first week in June every year in Mankato, Minnesota. Roger looked forward to showing his Corvette with its new tires and wheels. He knew that several others from Madison would be exhibiting in Mankato. Since it was less than two hundred miles from Roger's garage to the show site, he would drive his Corvette there, but others from South Dakota preferred to trailer their cars to Mankato. Em'ly didn't want to drive her '55 that far. She owned a heavy-duty pickup truck and an enclosed trailer specifically designed to carry the Corvette to shows. Ben would accompany her and assist with the driving and with loading and unloading the car.

Because he was the most familiar with Minnesota roads and the show site, Roger led the way with Em'ly's truck and trailer following. The mini-caravan traveled only about an hour before stopping for breakfast at a tiny café on Highway #14. Roger knew that it served the best biscuits and gravy in Minnesota. The three travelers parked and approached the café eagerly as if they were starved prisoners.

They sat on stools at the counter so as to be closer to the food. The biscuits were as large as land mines and the link sausages were as big as brats. Nevertheless, Roger ordered extra sausages. They ate like wild tigers that did not expect another meal for a week.

Ben Flowers pushed his empty plate away from him. "These biscuits and sausages are the best I've ever eaten. I had some in Dallas that

I thought were good, but these are better...
and they're certainly larger."

Em'ly said, "I thought everything was
supposed to be bigger in Texas."

"I was disappointed with lots of things
down there."

Roger asked, "When were you in Dallas?"

"I attended a computer school for executives
about six months ago. I was down there when
Gordy was killed. The school where I studied
was really in Las Colinas—just north of Dallas.
The word 'studied' might not be too accurate
for what we did. The school was more like a
social club, and we sat around drinking coffee
and joking most of the day. At any rate, there
were great restaurants in Las Colinas and in
Irving, next door. The nightlife in downtown
Dallas was wonderful."

Soon the trio was back on the road. They
drove for about three hours and reached North
Mankato. Roger turned off the highway and
followed city streets so that they could have

lunch at a pizzeria that Roger knew. They parked in a lot on the corner and walked to Dino's New York Style Pizzeria. As they entered, they seemed to swim in a warm sea of sweet scents—oregano, beef, and tomato. They ordered three large pizzas, and they planned to share with one another.

"Roger, did you say that you once lived here in North Mankato?" Em'ly asked.

"Yes. I spent my formative years here. I worked in a gas station just down Range Avenue there. I sometimes worked the midnight to 8:00 a.m. shift, and I got to know all the police in town. They would often swing into the station in the middle of the night and want to chat just to breakup their tedious shift, and I enjoyed talking with them.

"One night I was sitting in the police car gossiping with the policeman that I knew well, and as we rambled on, I took the handcuffs off the shotgun where they were hanging, and casually tapped one cuff on the side of one of my fingers, it spun around and locked on my finger. I pulled it off and tapped it on my finger over and over again as we talked. Then I absent-mindedly tapped one cuff on the side of my wrist, and, of course, it locked. I asked the policeman for the key, and he looked confused and said he didn't have it, but he could get one from another officer. Just then a call came over the radio for him to answer, and I had to get out of the car.

"There I stood in front of the gas station with a pair of handcuffs hanging from my left wrist. I stuffed the dangling end under my coat and went inside. Soon a car came in for gas. A man I had never seen before wanted his tank filled. I put the hose in his tank, and as I cleaned the windshield, I stretched out my left arm, and kerjang, bang—the handcuffs swung out from under my coat and bumped against the windshield. The driver stared at them, and immediately rolled up his window. He paid me by rolling down his window about half an inch and extending a twenty, and he told me to keep the change. He quickly drove away with several backward glances. He obviously thought that an escaped convict was running the station, as if the first thing an escapee would do is find a place to pump gas! Before any other customers arrived, another policeman drove in, and amid a lot of laughter and joking at my expense, he unlocked the cuffs and drove off with them—grinning at me."

The pizza was delivered to their table as Ben and Em'ly laughed. They ate a slice of each pizza and agreed that Em'ly's choice of Canadian bacon and pineapple was the best, although Roger's triple beef with dill pickle was excellent. Ben's choice of seven cheeses had some very bitter cheese, and he didn't finish it.

They arrived at the rolling meadows on the edge of town that was the site of the show just before the deadline of noon. The bright

June sun was directly overhead, and it was warm. This was a big show. A space equal to a city block was devoted to Corvettes. Roger parked at the end of a long row of modified Corvettes. Em'ly and Ben parked their truck and trailer across the street and drove the copper '55 into the meadows and parked diagonally behind Roger. As she jumped out of her car, Em'ly waved to Roger.

Because she had trailered her car to the show, Em'ly had only dusting and a little touchup polishing to do to make her car ready for judging. While she worked, she sent Ben to discover where to buy cool drinks for them.

Roger had much more work to do to put his car in show condition. He had scrubbed the brake dust from the wheels and tires and he was applying tire dressing when Em'ly walked over. "I am an expert at removing bugs," she said. "I'll start with the front end and continue with the windows."

"Thanks a million. I appreciate the help," Roger said as he continued to polish his chrome wheels. "Em'ly, give me some advice. I'd like to buy an early Corvette, a C1, and restore it and show it. What year car would you advise me to buy?"

Em'ly thought a moment as she sprayed foam window cleaner over the bugs on the front of Roger's car. "Well, they fall into four categories. If I had it to do over, I would avoid '53 to '55 simply because parts are so costly and difficult to find. The parts are listed in catalogs, but when you try to order them, you are told they are out of stock, or, worse yet, you receive them and find that they are different from the original equipment. Parts for the '56 and '57 cars are a little easier to get, but I would recommend '58 to '60. For some reason, the '61 and '62 cars are in fashion just now and are way over priced."

Roger nodded. "I like the '58 to '60. They are the last Corvettes to have the tail lights molded into the fenders, and I like the symmetrical smooth curves."

"And the pastel colors are cool."

"Actually, they are. They are so different from today's bright colors."

By the time Em'ly had finished the front of Roger's Corvette and had polished his windows, he had gone over the paint with a duster and with detail spray. She stood next to Roger as the two of them surveyed the car. Roger found several spots on the paint to touch up, and Em'ly went over half of the windshield again. Ben appeared next to the car and handed each of them a paper cup filled with cold lemonade. The three walked back to Em'ly's copper car and stood looking up and down the rows of cars. She had more than a dozen first-generation Corvettes of all years and colors competing against her car.

"That white Corvette is sure shiny and well polished," Ben said. "It looks like your car, Em'ly. Why would it be in the row with the modified Corvettes?"

"That's a new, modified car," Roger said. "It is called the 1953 Commemorative Edition Corvette. It is very rare—almost a one-off. It is made to look like a 1953 body, but it has a modern engine and running gear. It's easy to identify this model—notice the graceful flow of the front fenders over the wheels and how the hood dives between those fenders—the 1953 didn't look like that. Also notice that it has fifth-generation wheels exactly like mine. That particular car is owned by Darrell Yorick, and you'll notice that he is a compulsive polisher." They strolled over to look at the unique car.

The car's owner looked up from applying leather conditioner to the red interior as they approached. "Hi, Darrell," Roger said.

"Hey. How are you guys? Em'ly, I noticed your award-winning copper car as I drove in." He pulled a clean terrycloth towel from his bag and continued to work on his seats as they talked.

"I like your car," Ben said.

"Well, thank you. Not everyone agrees with you. Some people say my car is neither fish nor fowl, neither a historic car nor a thoroughly modern one. But I like it." He glanced up and smiled at them and then resumed buffing the seats.

A moment later, Darrell Yorick continued as if he were a pot boiling over. "I love this car, and it cost me a fortune, an absolute fortune, and I always put it in top show condition. I should be winning trophies in every show, but I'm not. It makes me mad! Really mad!" He stood glaring at them. He certainly was not at all embarrassed at his outburst.

"I'm sorry," Em'ly said. Not knowing what else to say, she turned and walked away, and her brother and Roger followed her. They walked slowly toward Em'ly's car without speaking.

They stood next to the copper car, looking back at Yorick and his car in the distance.

"He acts as if it is our fault that he's not winning," Roger said.

Em'ly nodded. "About a year ago, when I was still showing my PT Cruiser, that man and Gordy were having words at a show. As I walked up to them, Yorick said something similar to what he said just now. When he walked away, Gordy laughed and said Yorick was a harmless, frustrated banker. Now I wonder if he's dangerous."

Ben looked alarmed. "Should I go back to the truck and get my gun?"

"You carry a gun in the truck?" Roger asked.

"Well, I bought a .38 revolver in Dallas to have for protection. I put it in the glove compartment of the truck when we left Madison, just in case we wanted it."

"I think you can leave it where it is."

It was interesting to compare the judging of the two friends' cars. Since Em'ly's car was a restored Corvette, the team of five judges consulted a list of standards and checked off each item on their lists. They leaned into the engine bay and crawled under the car from the sides, back, and front. They rolled around on the floor and looked under the dash panel. They were very concerned about the numbers on the engine parts. Only one judge evaluated Roger's modified Corvette. He seemed to focus on the overall impression first, and then he studied the engine chrome, the wheels, the interior, and the mirrors and carpet in the trunk. He wrote down the scores when he was done and moved on.

After the judging, Roger strolled past all of the Corvettes. He talked to the owners of most of the first-generation cars. He was surprised to notice how many Corvettes in the show were red. He had studied the published Corvette paint color statistics, and he knew red was a popular color, but apparently red was an even more popular with exhibitors. He asked if the cars were for sale, and only one of the owners said he would consider selling, and the price quoted for a rather average car was outrageously high.

Late in the afternoon, under the hot sun, the trophies were announced. Roger was happy to receive the award for the best modified Corvette. He could see Yorick standing in the distance scowling. Em'ly won overall first place for Corvettes. She bounded up to accept the trophy with the energy that was characteristic of her. The ominous behavior of Yorick seemed to have been put out of her mind.

CHAPTER 6

W hen Roger saw the sheriff the day after they returned from Mankato, he asked, "Did you get deputies to keep an eye out for the safety of Em'ly?"

"Yes, but we don't have enough deputies to do a very good job of it."

"It may be comforting to know that her brother, Ben, seems to be accompanying her to shows, and he keeps a gun, a .38 revolver, in his glove compartment."

"I suppose when a brother is killed, the others in the family are bound to be on edge. I hope Ben doesn't do something stupid."

Having seen many nice early Corvettes at the Mankato show, Roger wanted to buy a C1 even more than he had previously. He remembered the casual comment by Professor Whelk that a man in her hometown of New Canaan, Connecticut, had a first-generation Corvette that he was trying to sell. Roger wanted to know more about that car. He looked up the phone number of its owner, Tom Weed, and called the hardware store that he owned.

Mr. Weed answered the phone, and when he learned that the caller was interested in buying his collector car rather than seeking information about rain gutters, his tone changed markedly. Yes, certainly, he did have a Corvette he wanted to sell. It was a 1960 Tasco Turquoise survivor with fewer than 40,000 original miles. It had not undergone a complete restoration, but it had been well maintained.

Roger asked the price, and found it reasonable, perhaps a little high. He explained that he lived halfway across the country from Tom but said that he very much wanted to look at this Corvette. The two men agreed that Roger would drive to New Canaan the following week and would stop on Saturday to see the car.

"I'll be working at the hardware store, Dr. Strong. Please ask for Mr. Weed."

Roger wondered why Tom was using such formal forms of their names. Had he offended him?

Even pulling a trailer behind his Hummer, Roger thought he could drive to Connecticut in two days—two long days. Early on the following Saturday, Roger drove north on the Merritt Parkway and turned off on South Avenue which took him into downtown New Canaan. It was a wonderful town with neat, uniform colonial storefronts. When he asked for directions, he found that he was only two blocks away from Weed and Duryea Hardware.

He walked into the store and saw a young man wearing a red shirt with "Weed and Duryea" printed on it. He was helping a woman select a shovel. "This model is designed for use in a professional nursery, and it is called The King of Spades," he said and chuckled at the hardware-store humor.

"Excuse me. Is Tom Weed here?"

"Mister Weed is in the back by the nails." He emphasized "Mister."

Roger walked to the back of the store and found a tall, thin man in a red shirt standing in front of bins of nails. He seemed to be counting them.

"Mr. Weed?"

The man in the red shirt put an open hand in the air and continued counting. Roger waited.

"Eight hundred and seven. There." He stood back and looked at Roger. "I presume that you are Dr. Strong."

"Yes."

"We sell nails by weight, but I find that it keeps my mind sharp to count them." He brushed the dust from his palms, and the two men shook hands. "So, Dr. Whelk, my high school classmate told you that I want to sell my Corvette. You are employed with her?"

"Er, yes."

Mr. Weed laughed. "I am not at all surprised that you hesitate to admit that you know her. I kinda liked her, but she always was a spitfire who offended most of the people she came into contact with."

Roger smiled and remained silent as Mr. Weed laughed heartily. After a moment, he coughed and regained his formal composure again. He said, "Let us proceed to view the Corvette."

As they drove in Mr. Weed's spotless white Cadillac, he said, "There are forty-one maple trees on this road. I sometimes take a different route home, and there are thirty-nine maple trees that way. Isn't it interesting that the count of maple trees is so similar?"

Roger replied that he would never have guessed.

Sensing Roger's lack of interest in maple trees, Mr. Weed changed the subject. "Dr. Whelk was in town for a school reunion a few months ago, and she wanted to buy something from me, and when she and I went to my house to get it, she saw the Corvette and we talked briefly about it. If you buy the car, I suppose I will owe her a finder's fee."

They followed a series of winding roads until they turned into a driveway almost hidden by the heavy foliage, and Roger saw a clearing with neatly mowed grass and a large stone house. Mr. Weed parked in his circular driveway and the two of them got out of the Cadillac, and Mr. Weed led the way to a garage behind the main house and opened the overhead door. He slowly removed a thick felt cover from a turquoise Corvette. The proud owner took a duster from a cabinet, and lightly dusted the car as he described it.

"It's an early 1960 model. The Vehicle Identification Number indicates that it was number 903 of more than ten thousand produced that year. As you see, it has white coves and is painted Tasco Turquoise—and that was the second rarest color in 1960. Only 635 turquoise Corvettes were made in 1960. The paint, trim, and interior have been carefully maintained, and they are all original. It has the optional wide wheels and has one of the higher horsepower engines."

Roger walked around the Corvette several times, and he opened both doors and looked at the seats and dash. He sat in the car and examined the steering wheel, gauges, and radio. He unlatched the hood and lifted it.

"I don't know a lot about engines," Mr. Weed said, "but I assume that this is the original 283 cubic-inch engine. It has a four-speed manual transmission. I think that the original valve covers have been replaced with those aftermarket finned aluminum covers. I looked at another 1960 at a show, and it had painted stamped steel valve covers. But the rest of the engine should be original."

"Do you mind if I jot down a few numbers?"

"No, I expected that you would do that." He handed Roger a pad of paper and a flashlight.

Roger craned his neck to see the numbers on the rear of the block of the engine. The casting date code was J119, which meant it was cast on October 11, 1959. That was an appropriate date for a correct engine in an early 1960 model Corvette. He wrote down the block casting number and the engine number, and he would check them later.

"It's interesting that the intake manifold has six bolts on each side," Mr. Weed said. "And look, the exhaust manifold also has six bolts on each side."

"Hmmm," Roger answered. At least at that moment, he was not too interested in counting bolts. He removed the two wing nuts on the large air cleaner and jotted down the numbers on the two Carter four-barrel carburetors. He knew that there were two engines available in 1960 that had carburetors, and he could tell from the Carter numbers that this was the engine with higher horsepower. The tachometer redline of 6500 also indicated the higher-performance carbureted engine.

He carefully put the air cleaner back in place. "Of course the fiberglass body does not rust, but is there any rust on the frame?"

"Almost none. Here, slide under the car on this cardboard and look at the frame."

Roger looked at the frame rails on the sides of the car. They were indeed clean and free from any but the most trivial hints of rust. He looked under the back of the car at the rear cross member—he knew that the wheels kicked up water and dirt on that cross member, and if there was any rust on the frame, it would be there. It was solid and had only superficial surface rust.

"Can we start the car and perhaps take it for a drive?"

"Dr. Strong, please don't be offended, but I must ask if you are really serious about buying this car."

He was offended, but he tried to control his reply. "I drove two full days to get here—and pulling an empty trailer! I would say I'm serious."

"Don't be angry. Calm down. I'll get the keys."

When Mr. Weed went into his house, Roger consulted a reference book about Corvette numbers that he had brought with him. Yes, the numbers were correct—as far as they went. At some point during the 1960 production year, a part of the vehicle identification number, called the VIN derivative, was added to the end of the engine number on Corvettes. This engine did not have a VIN derivative, but that absence would be expected on an early production model like this one. The engine suffix code of CU indicated two Carter four-barrel carburetors and a high-lift cam.

"This car has had limited, pampered use," Mr. Weed said as he returned and sat in his Corvette. The engine started quickly and it purred almost silently. He got out of the car, and Roger was waved into the driver's seat. He slowly pulled out of the driveway and headed down the road they had just driven. He shifted carefully, and he took curves at a moderate speed. He was looking for a car to fully restore, not a car to race, and he needed to know only that everything worked as it should. It was a perfect summer day, and Roger was driving the ideal car for that day.

When Roger returned, he shut off the car and got out and walked around it again. He looked carefully at the bumpers and large toothy grill. The chrome was good, but not perfect. The bright work around the coves was also good, but not perfect. The taillight lenses were clouded, but they were easy to replace. The original paint of the car was probably its best feature, but it was half a century old, and it showed signs of its age.

The two men talked about money. Roger made an offer below the asking price. It was rejected, but the asking price was lowered. Roger made a higher offer, and after a delay, it was accepted—with the condition that the money be electronically transferred prior to removal of the car. They shook hands. Roger took out his cell phone. "I will phone my bank and authorize the transfer, and while that's happening, let's go back into town so that I can get my truck and trailer."

About an hour later, Roger was loading a wonderful 1960 Corvette into his trailer. He had its title and a bill of sale in his pocket.

"Thank you, Mr. Weed."

"It has been a pleasure, Dr. Strong." He patted his pocket where he had a printed notice of the bank transfer. "It was certainly fortuitous that Dr. Whelk happened to see the Corvette in my driveway when she came over here to purchase that gun from me."

"She bought a gun from you?"

"Yes, it was a small .22 automatic that my wife had owned."

"Why did Rebecca—Dr. Whelk—want a gun?"

"I don't know. At the school reunion, she and I were talking about these being dangerous times. I mentioned that my wife once carried a .22 automatic, and now that she was gone, it was locked away. Dr. Whelk asked me if it was for sale, and I sold it to her."

Mr. Weed was silent a moment. "I later though that I shouldn't have sold the gun to her. Rebecca and I happened to be sitting at an isolated table toward the end of the reunion cocktail hour. She had quickly drunk quite a few drinks, and she started complaining about her fellow faculty back home. She said something about wanting to go out in a spectacular way. Perhaps she would shoot all the professors at a meeting and then shoot herself.

"But probably I didn't hear her correctly … I don't know…" He trailed off.

Dr. Strong looked serious and thoughtful, but he turned and saw his newly-purchased Corvette in his trailer, and everything else faded from his mind. As he lifted and locked the tailgate and got into his Hummer, a smile spread from ear to ear. Several times as he stopped to fill up with gas on the way home, he opened the trailer and grinned at his new car.

CHAPTER 7

Because he knew that he would find some assistance helpful in unloading his new Corvette, Roger had phoned Joey Bucket and asked to meet him at his garage when he returned. Roger could have unloaded the car without help, but he wanted to show it off to someone. When he pulled his Hummer and trailer into his driveway, the tall sheriff was waiting.

Roger jumped out of his truck and waved to Joey to join him at the rear of the trailer, and he opened the tailgate. "Ta-da! Look at that beautiful first-generation Corvette that

I'll make into a car rated Top Flight by the National Corvette Restorers Society!"

When the new treasure was safely parked in Roger's comfortable garage, each of the men walked around the car looking at it from every angle. Roger pointed out the strong features of the Corvette, and he noted some of the things that he would have to restore.

"It's certainly different from your yellow Corvette."

"Yes." As he walked around the car, Roger could hardly contain his excitement. "I believe that I am going to do a complete frame-off restoration—although the previous owner, Mr. Weed, didn't seem to think it needed it." He looked away from the car.

"By the way, Joey, I learned something interesting in Connecticut. You know that Rebecca Whelk told me about this car. She said that she had noticed it in her hometown of New Canaan when she was there for a school reunion. The man who sold me the

Corvette, Mr. Weed, said that she happened to see the car when she came to his house to buy a .22 automatic from him."

"Really? Why did she want a gun?"

"That's what I asked, but he didn't know."

Both men were silent a moment. "You said you would do a complete frame-off restoration."

"Yes, I think so."

"You will take the body off the frame, and put it aside and restore the frame, and then put the body back?"

"Yes."

"Then why don't you call it a body-off restoration?"

"I don't invent these terms. I simply use them." Roger grinned.

The next day was a school day, and although Roger would rather have pulled on jeans and a T-shirt and stayed home and cleaned and inspected his new car, he put on a tie and sport coat and trudged off to his campus. He sat at his desk preparing for a lecture. He turned in his office chair and tossed a book on top of a stack of books, and the stack teetered and tumbled to the floor. He needed another bookcase in his office. Phyllis in his college office had told him that Arts and Sciences did not have any unused bookcases, but she thought that the Business School had a number of them that were in storage. After his class, he walked to the next building and into the Business office.

Dr. Susan Mendenhall was the acting dean since the death of Bill Tyler. She had wanted to be a dean for most of her career. She had applied for a dean's position at other universities, but she had not received any job offers, and suddenly she became a dean at her own university, and she was very happy with her new title. She was standing near the door talking to the secretary when Roger entered.

"And another thing," she said. "I would like this office painted green. I have always thought that a business school office should look like the color of money!" She turned and almost ran into her visitor. "Hey, Roger, who let you out of the arts building?"

"Hi, Susan. Dean Jefferson lets us out once a month—if we promise to annoy the faculty in the Business School." Both of them smiled at the pleasantries that had a grain of truth. "I am here to beg a favor. Do you have a bookcase that you are not using that I could put in my office?"

"Actually, we have a million bookcases in storage, and you would be doing us a favor by taking one of them. Talk to Dusty Rhodes, the custodian of the building, and tell him I said you should take any bookcase you like. He is probably loafing in his supply room in the basement. I'm late for a meeting." Dr.

Mendenhall scooted past Roger and walked quickly down the hallway.

As Roger plodded down the steep stairs in the old building, he mused that every man he had ever known named "Rhodes" had the nickname of "Dusty." He wondered if the man he was about to see thought it was a clever name. The sounds of country-western music were coming from a door at the end of the hall. Roger knocked on the door and looked in. He saw a chubby young man wearing a dirty blue work shirt with the name "Dusty" embroidered on it. He was leaning back in an old office chair with his feet on a beat-up surplus desk. He quickly sat up and pulled his feet down and shut off the music when he saw Roger.

The room was clearly a janitor's supply room with its characteristic odor—perhaps from the oil on the many large mops leaning together in one corner. A metal storage rack held cleaning supplies and bundles of paper towels. Dusty had given the room a personal touch with his radio and coffee cup on the desk and by hanging a large poster that announced, "I am a proud member of the National Rifle Association."

"Dr. Mendenhall told me to talk with you, and you would help me find a bookcase that I can put in my office."

"Oh, so Susan thinks that I have nothing better to do than find pieces of furniture for her. She is no better than the last dean." He stood up and motioned with one hand, "Come on." He led the way into an adjacent room that was filled to the ceiling with desks, chairs, and bookcases. They were stacked every which way, and looked as if they would tumble down if any one of them were disturbed.

Roger saw a dark oak bookcase near the door, and he thought it could be pulled out fairly easily. "What if I used this one?"

"I don't know—that's solid oak."

"She said to tell you that I could use any one I wanted."

"I suppose she did—the dictator."

Roger started to pull the bookcase toward the door. "Could you hold this desk while I pull the bookcase?" Reluctantly, Dusty assisted. When it had been moved away from the other furniture, Roger saw that it was exactly what he needed.

"I don't know how you're going to get it over to your building."

A voice came from behind them. "Are you finding what you need, Roger?" It was Dean Mendenhall.

"Ah,…yes I am. You surprised me. I thought you were on your way to a meeting."

"It was cancelled. Dusty, you'll load Roger's bookcase on the elevator and take it over to the arts building, won't you?"

"I'll be happy to do that," he said without a hint of sincerity.

As Dr. Mendenhall turned and walked away, Dusty made a face toward her back. He was silent as he and Roger moved the bookcase from one building to another. Roger thanked him, and he mumbled and grumbled as he returned to his building. Roger pushed the bookcase back against the wall. He would load his books on it later.

He had to get ready to teach his literary criticism class—a course with rather difficult abstract content. He had hit upon a method of teaching the course that both he and his students enjoyed. He appeared in the classroom at the start of the hour pretending to be the author that students had been reading. He would try to imitate the characteristic dress of the author and quote some of the better-known writings, and then invite questions.

The classroom door swung open to reveal to the waiting students a man wearing a black academic robe with a long colorful hood draped down his back. He had a mortarboard cap on his head. "I am Matthew Arnold, your guest speaker today." He strode into the room. "I am a professor of poetry at Oxford and I am also an inspector of schools. However, you know me best as the author of essays—including my 'Preface to Poems, 1853' which I understand you read for today. I will briefly summarize it."

He talked about the essay as he marched back and forth across the front of the room in a theatrical way. Then with a swish of his robe, he stood facing his students and demanded, "What questions do you have?"

At first the students were a little stunned with his bravado performance, and they sat silent. Then a scholarly-looking young man in the front row tentatively raised his hand. "Sir, can a poem be written on any topic? About any subject?"

"Good question! The answer is yes. A poem can be written about anything.

However, the real question is whether a poem is interesting. Now, what is *not* interesting is that which is vaguely conceived and loosely drawn; a representation which is general, indeterminate, and faint, instead of being particular, precise, and firm. A poem must inspirit and rejoice the reader."

Roger was on a roll quoting Arnold, and he continued. "Poetical works belong to the domain of our permanent passions and therefore they should have appropriate subjects that are significant actions. It is a pity that power should be wasted, and that the poet should be compelled to impart interest and force to his subject, instead of receiving them from it, and thereby doubling his impressiveness."

At the end of the hour, Roger and Mathew Arnold performed a deep stage bow and thanked the students for their attention.

CHAPTER 8

On an unusually hot and humid summer afternoon, Roger was mowing his lawn and bumped the mower against a tree near his house. A moment later he felt a sharp pain on his wrist, and when he looked down, he saw that a wasp had stung him. He brushed the wasp off and backed away from the tree. He had received a sting in almost the same place on his wrist the last time he had mowed the lawn near that tree. He peered through the branches of the tree and sure enough—there was a large wasp's nest hanging from a branch. The queen wasp must have heard the mower approaching and issued an order to one of her soldiers: "Go sting that mowing jerk in the wrist!"

When Roger finished mowing and had put his mower in the garage, he saw his neighbor, Mr. Bickett, in his yard. He was a retired farmer and might know how to get rid of a wasp's nest.

"I can deal with wasps because I've done it before. This is what we'll do." Mr. Bickett spoke with confidence, and Roger was surprised that he had immediately put himself into a position of helping with the project and was not simply giving advice. "We'll wait until after sunset (wasps always go inside their nest at sunset and they sleep there until dawn). Then I'll half fill a large bucket with DDT, and you can jam a cork plug in the opening of the nest, and cut off the branch it is attached to. It will fall into the bucket of DDT, and I'll quickly cover it with a tarp. After a day or two, the wasps will all die, and we'll throw out the nest.

"I'll meet you out here tonight. Remember to wear clothing to protect you—thick clothing with long sleeves. I'm going to wear a parka and wrap a scarf over my face. Don't forget to wear boots."

As it grew dark, Roger saw Mr. Bickett crossing into his yard carrying a large bucket and pulling a tarp behind him. His motion was stiff and clumsy because he was wearing so many layers of clothes. Because the evening was warm and humid, Roger was reluctant to wear a parka and gloves, but he did put them on. He wore two pairs of jeans and galoshes that were too large for him. Roger joined his similarly-dressed neighbor on the lawn. They saw no wasps. They spoke in hushed whispers so as not to disturb the sleeping insects. The bucket was placed under the nest, and Roger gently inserted a cork from a wine bottle into the hole on the bottom of the nest. He started to saw off the branch holding the nest, and Mr. Bickett was ready to pull the heavy tarp over the bucket when the nest fell into it. Roger's saw was not too sharp, and he was making slow progress with the branch, when suddenly the branch broke, and at the same moment, the cork dropped out of the hole. The air was filled with wasps.

"Run...Run!" Mr. Bickett yelled, and both men ran as fast as they could around the house into the front yard. They stopped and warily looked back, fearing that the wasps would follow them.

A car pulled up and stopped on the street behind them. Roger glanced around and saw his friend Joey Bucket getting out of the car. When Joey saw the two men on the lawn, he stopped and stared in wonder. It was a very warm evening, and these two grown men stood in the middle of Roger's front lawn wearing heavy parkas, gloves, and boots, and the older man even had a scarf wound across his face. Both men gave frequent nervous looks behind them.

"What's the problem?" Joey asked as he approached.

Roger attempted to explain, "We were getting rid of a wasp's nest, but the plug fell out, and we had to run."

Mr. Bickett said, "I'll bet the wasps lined up one behind another and pushed the cork out."

After a few minutes they carefully walked back to the bucket. They did not see any wasps, and they discovered that the nest had landed in the bucket when the branch broke. Mr. Bickett gingerly pulled the tarp over it, and he told Roger that he shouldn't fool with it for at least a day or two.

Roger pulled off his gloves and parka; he was soaked with perspiration. He repeatedly thanked his helpful neighbor who waved over his shoulder as he trundled home still wearing his heavy clothing. Then Roger and Joey wandered back to Roger's garage where he described the experience fully. Joey, naturally, thought it was very funny. Roger did not. He changed the topic of conversation as soon as he could. "I have a new beautiful oak bookcase in my office."

Joey would have preferred to continue discussing Roger's adventure with the wasps, and he didn't find the subject of bookcases exactly engrossing, but he politely asked, "How did you get it?"

"I talked to Susan Mendenhall—you know her—the new dean in Business. She is certainly taking a command and control attitude in that college. 'Jump, jump…snap to it.' Anyway, she told me to get the bookcase from the janitor, Dusty Rhodes—you probably know him too."

"I talked with him and with Dr. Mendenhall when we found Dean Tyler's body." The sheriff was thoughtful and much more interested.

"Dusty helped me move the bookcase to my office—he didn't want to help, but Susan made him do it." Roger laughed. "I remember that he made a face at her back."

"So he doesn't like her?"

"No. He said she is a dictator."

"Is she?"

"Well, she likes being a dean—it's what she wanted for a long time. And she seems to enjoy giving orders. In fact, now that I reflect on it, she likes giving orders a little too well."

"Did Dusty like his previous dean, Dr. Tyler?"

"No. He spoke about him with similar contempt."

"So you had conversations with a woman who wanted to be a dean and with a man who does not like deans. Is that right?

"I guess so. You are thinking that both Susan and Dusty had motives for killing Dean Tyler?"

"That would be putting it too strong," the sheriff said. "Far too strong. The key word is 'thinking.' We are simply thinking."

"Speaking of thinking, I have all kinds of major and minor issues to think through as I restore this new 1960 Corvette of mine."

"Tell me about one of the minor things. I don't feel up to considering a major issue."

"I would say that the hubcaps are a minor issue. I have had polished wheels with no hubcaps on my cars for decades, so this is something new for me to consider. Now, my 1960 Corvette has the optional wide wheels—'wide' indeed, they are only a half inch wider than the standard wheels. And they are only a fraction of the width of the wheels I had on my T-bucket hot rod. Anyway, you will notice that the car has rather nice looking stainless steel hubcaps that are correct for 1960. They have the slots around the edge as they should, and they have the ice-blue hue of the original equipment rather than the yellowish look of replacement hubcaps. They are usually called full wheel covers to distinguish them from the small dog-dish hubcaps that came on the wide wheels. The problem is that these wide wheels should have the small hubcaps."

"So, change the hubcaps—what is the problem?"

"I like the full wheel covers much better. And I like the wide wheels, and I don't want to change them."

"What are you going to do?"

"I think I will keep the full wheel covers with the wide wheels, and when the car is judged by an NCRS team, I will see if I get a deduction."

"I would change the wheels—you said the ones that go with the wheel covers are only slightly narrower."

Roger nodded. "I will do that if I must. And the tires present another problem. For the best ride and performance, the car should have radial tires rather than the original bias-ply tires. Now, there are some radial tires that are supposed to look like the vintage whitewall tires the car came with, but they are really not too similar and wouldn't fool any judge."

"That's an easy one. Go with the old bias-ply tires. You are not going to make repeated trips to California in this car. You can live with the performance of original tires."

Joey got up to leave. "You said that Dr. Mendenhall is now the Dean of Business. Is it usual to select a new dean from the current faculty?"

"Strictly speaking, her title is Acting Dean, and it is almost always the case that the acting position is filled from current faculty since it must be done quickly so that the college can continue to operate. There will be a national search for a permanent dean, but the person currently serving in the position always has an inside track to be selected for it—assuming that she wants to fill it—which Susan certainly does."

"I want to follow up on what you told me about her and about Dusty Rhodes. I would like you to be with me when I talk to them. Can we do that next week?"

"Well, I must check to see how my wasps are doing, but I can probably make time for your interview."

CHAPTER 9

Roger had never entered two cars in one show, and he looked forward to showing both of his Corvettes in the Village Car Show. He wanted to put his 1960 in a show to see how it would do in competition prior to his restoration of it. His 2004 Millennium Yellow Corvette had been his show car for several years, and he didn't see why he should stop entering it simply because he now owned another Corvette.

He cleaned and prepared his 2004 as usual for a show, and then turned his attention to the 1960. First he vacuumed the seats with a machine he reserved for seats and then vacuumed the carpet with a different one. Then he went over the dash and seats with cleaner. He next washed the car. Since this was the first time Roger had washed it, he mixed some kerosene with the water to remove old dirt and grime—he wouldn't want to use kerosene every time he washed the car, but once wouldn't hurt, and it might be helpful. He went over every inch of it thoroughly and then rinsed it with distilled water and dried it with a blower and then with soft towels. He gave the paint and chrome several coats of carnauba wax. He had long ago substituted a synthetic clear coat for carnauba wax on his 2004, but synthetic did not seem appropriate for his 1960. He knew the carnauba would give a deep glow to the turquoise paint, and that's what he wanted rather than the highly reflective surface shine of a synthetic.

Roger used sugar water as tire dressing on the 1960 rather than the commercial dressing that he used on the 2004—he wanted it to leave a smooth dull black surface on the tires rather than a shiny black shine. He cleaned the glass twice, both inside and outside, with a foam cleaner and then went over the glass again with Windex to make it sparkle. He also used Windex to make the chrome as bright as possible. He stood back a few feet—the old car looked pretty good.

He had discovered some interesting things about his 1960 as he cleaned it. For example, the front fenders were not absolutely flat and level as they appeared at first glance, but they were slightly convex—Roger could feel the curve under his wash mitt. As a wise old car guy had told him, "You will learn more about your car the first time you wash it than you can ever learn by simply looking at it."

The Village Car Show was only three or four miles from Madison, so both cars could easily be driven to it. Joey Bucket had agreed to drive one of the Corvettes to and from the show, and he wanted to pilot the 2004, telling Roger that he liked it better because it would go faster. "I want to see if I can bury the speedometer at the 200 mark!" Roger immediately looked at Joey to be sure that he was joking, and the two set off with Roger's 1960 in the lead.

The Village was a replica of an early Midwest village, and the cars in the show were staged among the old buildings. This car show had a very different character from the Madison Car Show, although it took place only a few miles distant. Bitzer had been the director of the Village show for years. His grandfather had been a light porter who rushed here and there making deliveries, and the grandson had inherited many of his traits. Bitzer greeted Roger at the main entry for exhibitors.

"You have a new car, Roger. That's great!" He spoke very fast. "Quick, quick, quick. Back your Corvette into a space across from the blue T-bucket and park next to the red and white Corvette. Hurry up."

"Good morning, sheriff. Follow Roger and park next to him. Let's get a move on!"

There was almost an hour before the published starting time of the show, so there was no reason for Bitzer to urge them to rush, but that was his way. As Roger carefully backed his car onto the grass next to the red and white early Corvette, he recognized the car—it was a 1957 Corvette that had won several national awards and had been featured in several magazines. Roger wondered if the Village judges would automatically award it first place in the sports car category.

Despite his remark about the 2004 being able to go fast, Joey drove it very carefully. He backed the car up next to Roger at about one mile per hour. The two men got out of their cars and glanced around at the show. "I don't see Em'ly's copper Corvette," Joey said.

"I don't see it either. That's strange. There is Darrell Yorick and his interesting 53/03 Corvette. He is furiously polishing it, as usual.

Roger wore his lucky *Hot Rod Magazine* wristwatch, and he needed all the luck he could get. He had received the watch for free when he subscribed to the magazine—he had not realized that he would get anything other than the magazine itself, so he was surprised. He figured that it was good luck, and he wore it to shows. The first time he wore the watch, his car won the Best-in-Show trophy.

Although Joey claimed to know nothing about preparing a car to be exhibited and judged, he was very helpful. He used several polishing rags and lots of the highly-reflective detail spray to remove a few bug marks from the front of the 2004. Roger praised his work, but exhorted him to be sure the detail spray did not dry on the paint.

As the two were finishing, Joey said, "I like this large bag you carry your detailing stuff in. The clean rags and supplies are in the top section and in the pockets on the sides, and the bottom part is a compartment for the soiled rags. Where'd you get it?"

"It is called a Car Care Organizer Bag II, and I ordered it from Griot's Garage, an extremely top-end shop."

"La-dee-dah!" They both smiled.

Their neighbor, the owner of the award-winning 1957, stepped over and introduced himself. He wore a bright red and white Hawaiian shirt that reminded Roger of the shirts worn by the great hot rod builder Boyd Coddington. "I'm Carroll Pryo, and everyone calls me Pie."

"I'm glad to meet you—I'm Roger Strong, and this is Joey Bucket. Everyone calls him The Sheriff."

As Pie shook Joey's hand, he asked, "Why do they call you The Sheriff?"

"Because I'm the sheriff in this county."

"That's a good reason."

"However, no one really calls me The Sheriff—except my idiot friend here."

Pie grinned. "I have friends like that in Minneapolis. I like to give names to cars— mine is called Rosie, for obvious reasons—and my friends make fun of me. Your Millennium Yellow Corvette I would call The Sun because it looks like a glowing sun—beautiful paint and wonderful polish, sheriff."

"Actually, both of these Corvettes belong to Roger. I'm simply the designated driver of this one for today."

"I see. I would call this turquoise car The Turk. Nice survivor. I love the pastel color, and your coves are pure white—mine are beige by comparison. But, I don't see a copper 1955 that I was warned would kick my car's butt. Do you know such a Corvette?"

"Yes," Roger replied. "It is a perfect restoration that is owned by Em'ly Flowers —who is a friend of ours. We were just remarking that it is surprising that she's not exhibiting here today."

"Perhaps her absence will make those of us who are showing run-of-the-mill Corvettes look good, but I was looking forward to seeing that car."

"Are you talking about the Flowers '55?" Darrell Yorick had walked up as the men where chatting.

"Yes, we were." Roger introduced Darrell and Pie.

"Do you know why Em'ly isn't here?" Joey asked Darrell.

"No, I certainly don't!" Darrell Yorick said, starting. He looked at the sheriff for a moment as if he had been accused of something. "However," he said calmly, "I agree that the rest of us Corvette owners will have a chance in this show without her car."

As the four men stood talking, they could smell the mouth-watering aroma of burgers cooked over charcoal. Roger looked toward the food stand. "Let's get something to eat," he said, and Joey and Pie looked as if he were expressing exactly their innermost thoughts.

"I must finish polishing my car," Yorick said, and he turned and walked away.

Joey and Pie ordered standard burgers, Roger got a triple burger, and they ate their burgers as they slowly walked back toward their cars. They could see a man with a clipboard in the distance moving toward the Corvettes—a judge, almost certainly. As he worked his way nearer, Roger recognized him as the rookie judge who was a trainee at Jerry's show.

"Good day, Brayden," Roger said pleasantly as the judge moved in front of the Corvettes. He didn't seem to recognize Roger, but as he glanced at the chrome under the hood of Roger's 2004, his face lit up in recognition.

"Oh, hey. I thought at first that I didn't know you from Adam or Eve, but I remember that you were exhibiting this car at Jerry's All-Corvette show."

"Yes," the bulky former football player turned professor said, "but I certainly don't look like an Eve."

"Of course not, but I said, 'know you from Adam or Eve' because I think it is important to use inclusive language."

"I see." Roger felt like laughing, but he didn't want to insult the man who was about to judge his cars.

Brayden stood chatting a few minutes and then said, "I had better make a decision about these Corvettes…there is no use kicking it down the can."

Brayden examined several other Corvettes, and then Yorick's custom and Pie's 1957, and then Roger's 1960, and, finally, his 2004. He walked back and forth—apparently to compare features of each. He took a very long time looking very close at the 1960, and he seemed to know exactly what to inspect. He had been trained well.

"This decision is a hard boat to row," he murmured. At last, Brayden started writing on his clipboard and he added up the scores and looked satisfied with himself. He looked over at the men. "I'm sorry to be as slow as mole asses."

With the sun low in the sky, Bitzer called the exhibitors toward the food stand, and he quickly announced the trophy winners. Roger was pleased that his 2004 was the best modified Corvette since he assumed that it would be the only trophy he would win that day. He was surprised that his 1960 was awarded first place as the best restored Corvette. He was even more amazed to have it named the best sports car in the show. As he picked up his trophy, he noticed Yorick was shaking his head. Pie was very good-natured in offering congratulations to Roger. "It does Rosie good to have her see other cars honored."

Pie Pryo drove off in his 1957. He had parked his trailer at the motel, and he would load the car there and return to Minneapolis. Joey and Roger were putting the show supplies in their cars and were about to leave also when Brayden walked by them.

"Thanks for the honors, Brayden."

"Well, my best judgment was that your cars deserved them. I especially liked your 1960 survivor. The parts are not new, yet they shine as if they had been polished daily."

"You didn't deduct for the full wheel covers on the wide wheels?"

Brayden looked embarrassed. "Sometimes I can't see beyond the end of a hose," he said as he squatted down to look closer at one of the front wheels of the 1960. "No, these are the narrow wheels with the correct wheel covers." He stood up. "The wide wheels have no mounting provisions at the outer rim for the full wheel covers—these do. If you had the wide wheels, you would have to use the small dog-dish hubcaps."

Roger nodded. He was pleased because he liked the full wheel covers, and he wanted to keep them on the car.

"I have been studying to become an NCRS judge," Brayden said. "You might have deductions for an NCRS show, but for this event, your car is very nice and deserved the award."

"I want to ask you something, and if you can't answer, I'll understand," Roger said to Brayden. "Why did the 1953 Commemorative Edition Corvette not do better?"

"Well, I can't comment on the scores of any individual car, but I can state a general judging rule—the entire car should be free of dirt, grease, and grime. It would not matter how well polished the paint and seats are if the engine is greasy and the wheels are caked with brake dust. Everything should shine.

That's why they say that the whole is equal to the sun on its parts."

Roger thought that he understood. Yorick's Corvette was a wonderful car that deserved to win trophies, but, as compulsive as Yorick was about cleaning his interior and polishing the paint, especially the hood and fenders, he was ignoring other parts of the car that most exhibitors would routinely clean.

"Sometimes it is obvious," Brayden said, "that an exhibitor runs out of time to properly clean the car when the judge shows up. I always feel sorry for such a person, but it's a case of getting stuck holding the bag when the music stops."

When Joey and Roger had returned the two Corvettes to Roger's garage, Joey sat on the comfortable leather couch, watching Roger replenish the supplies in the show bags. Both men wanted to talk about the show.

"Did you expect Em'ly to enter her copper Corvette at this show?" Joey asked.

"Yes. I was very surprised that she wasn't there."

"Perhaps she was out of town."

"And speaking of being surprised, I was very surprised at how much our judge, Brayden, had learned since the first time I saw him as a judge. He has been well trained, and he has lots of knowledge. And I like that he certainly is not the least bit smug about his judging abilities.

"Brayden set me right about my wheels and wheel covers. Mr. Weed, the man who sold me the car, told me that it had the wide wheels. Well, as Brayden pointed out, they are not. In addition, Weed told me that the valve covers that were on the car were replacements, and they actually were the original covers— the seven-rib die-cast aluminum covers with 'Corvette' in high relief were on the higher performance models like this one. He didn't seem to know too much about his own car."

Looking a little bewildered with all the Corvette details, Joey announced that he was leaving. "Tomorrow let's stop and talk to Dean Mendenhall and Dusty Rhodes."

"Okay. I'll call her office to set a time."

CHAPTER 10

Thunderstorm clouds threatened on the horizon late in the afternoon as Sheriff Joseph Bucket and Dr. Roger Strong were shown into Dean Mendenhall's office. She waved toward two chairs, and when she closed the door to her office, she told the college secretary not to bother them. Both Joey and Roger noticed the overbearing tone she took with the secretary, and they glanced at one another.

"This is a temporary college office, sheriff, since the real office is sealed, and it's off limits to us. How much longer will it be sealed?

"Well, Dean Mendenhall, the office of Dean Tyler is a crime scene. We can't release it until our investigation is complete."

"When do you think that will be? I need that office."

"I don't know. Dean Tyler's office is—"

"It isn't Dean Tyler's office—it is the college office—the Office of the Business School."

"Okay. That office contains primary evidence of the murder, and it must be preserved."

"I have a good mind to pull down your tape and move into that office where I should be."

The sheriff learned forward. "Ma'am, if you did that, you would be guilty of interfering with a police investigation, and that is a felony and can result in a ten-year prison term." The voice of the sheriff was not loud, but its tone was intense.

Susan Mendenhall leaned back and laughed. "I'm joking, sheriff. I would never do such a thing. I respect law and order as much as you do."

The sheriff sat silent. He could see that he was understood. After a moment, Dr. Mendenhall continued. "But this is not what you wanted to talk to me about. What questions do you have?"

Joey looked at Roger. "The talk on campus," Roger said, "is that you have wanted to be a dean for some time. Is that true?"

"Well…yes, of course I want to move up in my chosen profession—I'm sure that you do, too."

"I haven't applied for deans' positions at other schools. Have you?"

"No, of course not. Well, perhaps one or two."

Sheriff Bucket nodded. "Where were you on the night that Dr. Tyler was killed?"

"What? Am I a suspect?"

"It's a routine question."

"I can't believe this! Because I am willing to step up and serve as a dean, you think I killed Bill Tyler! No good deed goes unpunished!"

"We have asked the same question of others."

Dr. Mendenhall glared at the sheriff. "On Sunday, I was at home all night—alone."

"I see."

"You don't believe me!"

"I simply acknowledged your answer."

"This meeting is done. Finished." She got up and held the door open.

Roger followed the sheriff out of the office and into the hallway. When they were alone, Roger said, "I thought that went well." He grinned. "I have always wanted to say that."

Joey was not amused. He looked thoughtful. "I learned a lot from that interview."

"Let's see if Dusty Rhodes is downstairs."

The two men found the lowest level of the building dark, and the supply room where Roger had found Dusty was silent and empty.

Joey turned on the light and walked around in the room. He glanced at the National Rifle Association poster and opened the drawers on the metal desk that Dusty used as a footrest. Something was heard rolling around in the back of an otherwise empty drawer. Joey took out a live .38 caliber round, and, after examining it, put it back in the drawer.

"Dusty probably went home hours ago," Roger said. "Most custodians start work very early, perhaps at 4:00 a.m. and quit for the day about noon. We would probably find him here tomorrow morning."

Under very dark clouds, Roger walked back to his office building. He gathered the books he needed to read that night and put them in a plastic bag. He looked out the window and saw that large drops of rain had started to fall. He grabbed his umbrella from the coat rack. When he pushed open the door of the building, the wind showered him with rain, and it swirled around him as he walked home.

He had all he could do to keep the umbrella over his head and prevent it from catching the wind and turning inside out. His shoes were wet immediately, and soon his pants legs were soaking, and even his sport coat was hit by rain. He wondered why he had bothered with the umbrella.

Thunder rumbled among the low, black clouds. Roger pushed open his back door and squeaked into his kitchen, and he dropped the open umbrella and stood dripping. "That is heavy rain," he thought. He changed clothes—leaving his wet clothing hanging on various open doors throughout the house.

With increased lightning overhead, Roger ran through the steady rain to his garage and stumbled inside. He was met with the sweet scents of car polish, leather dressing, and detailing spray. He looked back through the window in the door, and he noticed that the rain was so heavy that it was difficult to see the house next door. He looked around his comfortable garage and turned on all the halogen floodlights. It was warm, pleasant, and cozy in the garage. Almost instinctively, he started to dust his 2004 Corvette—thinking of it as the Glowing Sun, the name that Pie had given the car—and he polished it with detail spray. Through the garage windows, he could see the branches of the trees blown about, and he could hear the rain on the roof. The thunder continued to rumble and tumble in the distance. He enjoyed working in his garage when the weather was bad.

Early in the morning, Roger spotted Joey waiting for him in front of the business building, and the two of them went downstairs to talk with Dusty Rhodes. They found him coming out of his storage room.

"Are you here to get another bookcase?" he asked by way of greeting Roger.

"Not exactly. But if I do take one, I have brought help for the heavy lifting. You know Sheriff Bucket?"

Dusty didn't answer the question, but asked one of his own. "Do you want to talk to me?" He spoke with a tone that expressed his hope that they were just passing by.

"Yes," the sheriff said. He motioned toward the storage room. "Should we go inside and talk?"

Reluctantly, the janitor opened the door and the three men went inside and sat around Dusty's desk on beat-up chairs that were not wanted by anyone.

"The other day when I was here," Roger said, "you indicated that Dr. Susan Mendenhall was acting in a dictatorial manner as dean. Could you say a little more about her?"

"Am I in trouble with the police just because I criticized her?"

"No, of course not," Roger said. "We simply wanted to know why you said what you did."

"Well, she gives me orders ... and she is not my supervisor. The manager of the physical plant hired me ... she didn't. She wasn't even the dean when I was hired. Why should she give me orders?"

"The deans do have immediate management responsibilities for the buildings."

"Yes, but she marches me around as if I'm her personal servant."

"Can you give us an example?"

"Just this morning she wanted the carpet in her office vacuumed. I asked her if she was expecting visitors, and she said she was not."

"Was the carpet dirty?"

"Only a little." He looked at Roger and Joey as if his harsh opinion of her was thereby justified.

"I see," the sheriff said. "Was Dean Tyler different?"

"No, not at all. In fact, he was even worse. He told me that I should clean and dust the stairs! With students and faculty stamping up and down them all day, the stairs clean themselves!" Again, he had a look of vindication.

"Everyone wants to give me orders. The day before Dean Tyler was killed, I forgot to turn off the sprinklers. In the evening, I thought of them and came over to shut them off—the ground was soaked and the water had pooled on the sidewalks. As I was getting out of my truck, I saw the dean splashing up the sidewalk toward his office. I turned off the water, and noticed that Ben Flowers was picking his way through the water on the sidewalk. When I passed him, he said, 'You could turn off the water a little sooner next time!' As if he was my boss!"

Dusty stood up, and the other two did the same. "Do you want another bookcase or not? I have work to do."

Sheriff Bucket nodded toward the desk drawer where he had found the bullet. "What do you keep in there?"

"Nothing."

"Can we look?"

Dusty quickly yanked the drawer fully open, and the bullet clanked to the front. He looked at it and grinned. "How'd you know there was anything in there?"

"I have X-ray vision. Why is there a live round in your desk?"

"I'm a proud member of the NRA," he pointed to his poster, "and I sometimes go to the gun range after work and shoot. At one time, I kept my gun and ammunition in that drawer."

"You should keep your gun locked up."

"I do now. I keep it locked in my truck. I didn't realize that there was a round in the desk."

As Joey and Roger were walking out of the building, Roger looked at his friend, and the sheriff shrugged his shoulders as if to say, "Who knows about that guy."

CHAPTER 11

June ended with some of the hottest weather in years. Roger's office was in the oldest building on campus, and he loved that noble granite building, but it did not have central air conditioning. Instead, each office had a window air conditioner, most of them had been in place for years and years. Roger had kept his air conditioner running continuously for more than a week. It made so much noise that Roger joked that an unusually large Buick V8 engine powered it.

When he arrived at his office on Monday, he found a very attractive young lady waiting for him at his door. He noticed that she had

small tattoos on her neck and arms. "I am
your new office assistant, Dr. Strong. I'm Nell
Underwood." She smiled at him and tipped
her head to the side in a flirtatious way. Roger
welcomed Nell to her new position and the
two went into the cool office and sat down
and discussed her working hours. They had to
speak up in order for them to hear each other
over the roar of the air conditioner.

Roger looked at his watch. "I must teach a
class, but while I'm gone, please put all these
books that are on the floor onto that empty
bookcase. If you can organize them in some
way, I'd appreciate it."

When Roger returned to his office, he
found that the floor was clear of books and Nell
must have found a broom and swept it. The
books were neatly placed on the shelves of his
new bookcase. Roger scanned the titles of the
books that he knew so well. A dictionary was
next to an anthology of American literature
and a work of literary criticism; then he saw

a biography of Dickens side by side with a history of his county. "How did you organize the books?" he asked her.

"By color. My dad says that I have a good sense of color. You can see that your books are in order according to the colors of the spectrum—red, orange, yellow, green, blue, and violet. I put the black books before the red ones, and I put the white ones after the violet. I arranged the books on your other bookcase in the same way. I hope that's okay."

"Nell, that's ingenious. Thanks. Now all I need to do to find a book in my bookcase is remember its color. And you straightened that mess of papers on the window ledge, and you stacked the reams of paper together."

Looking rather pleased with her efforts, she said, "It's nothing."

Roger looked back toward his bookshelves with the rainbow of colors and smiled. "My books remind me of the range of bright colors on cars at a car show."

"I know that you have a wonderful yellow Corvette. Some day I'd like to own a car exactly like yours."

Roger smiled. "Perhaps you'll buy mine." He supposed that it was rather unlikely.

"I would like that!" She looked excited. "I had better go over to the physics lab for a class now, but I'll return at the same time for work tomorrow."

Roger smiled as she left the room. "Yes," he thought, "this Nell Underwood would be a good office assistant."

After his classes were finished for the day, Roger walked home—he was hungry. He changed into his car-working clothes and draped his school clothes over the bedroom door, and returned to his large kitchen. He would make grilled cheese sandwiches— he had grown up calling them toasted cheese sandwiches.

He knew that he used far too much butter on the sandwiches, but he didn't care. He put a heavy skillet on the stove, and put several pats of cold butter in it. While the pats were melting, he buttered four slices of bread and sliced cheddar cheese and Swiss cheese. He put the bread in the pan, buttered side down. While the slices were browning, he buttered the tops. He flipped the bread—adding more pats of butter under each of the slices of bread. He put multiple slices of cheddar and Swiss cheese on the toast and added a small dollop of sour cream and covered it with the two toasted bread slices. He turned the sandwiches once more.

When melted cheese started to ooze pleasantly out the sides of the sandwiches, Roger knew they were done. He put them on a plate and cut them diagonally. He moved his plate to the table along with a jar of sliced dill pickles. He opened each oozing sandwich and added cold pickles. The sandwiches were excellent. The tart dill taste perfectly complemented the blended cheese taste, and he liked the contrast in textures and temperatures. Something was missing. He got up and found a bag of potato chips and ate a few with his next sandwich. Perfect.

He cleaned his kitchen and headed for his garage. He needed to put gasoline in his 1960 Corvette. He drove to a nearby station, Ray's Service. He had worked there when he was a struggling undergraduate student. Ray seemed to have a lot of accidents, and Roger remembered one in particular.

Ray had contracted with a dairy to house one of its milk trucks in the lubrication bay of the station each night. As Roger and Ray were near closing every evening, they would fill the truck with gas, wash down the lubrication bay, and then drive the truck inside and lock up the station.

On a bitterly cold night, Ray had backed the truck up to the pump island and put the hose nozzle in the tank, started the pump, and slid the lever into a small notch in the handle to keep the gas flowing. The pump was designed to click off when the gas in the tank reached the tip of the nozzle. He knew that this nozzle did not always shut off properly, but it was far too cold to stand next to the truck and wait for it to fill.

Inside, behind the frost-covered windows, Ray watched Roger hose the concrete floor of the bay from side to side, and then he squeegeed the water toward the floor drain. Both men were proud of cleaning the floor until it was spotless every night. After about thirty minutes, Ray told Roger to go outside and top off the tank of the milk truck and drive it inside. When he walked toward the truck, Roger found that the nozzle had not shut off, and gas was running down the side of the truck onto the ground. The truck tank held only about twenty-five gallons, but the pump meter recorded over one hundred and fifty gallons delivered. As far as Roger could see, gasoline was flowing across the platform—it was flooded.

He shut off the pump and ran inside and yelled to his boss. When Ray looked out the door, he let out an agonizing yelp and told Roger to shut off all the electricity. The fire department was called, and very quickly numerous red trucks with flashing lights arrived and firemen and hoses were everywhere. The high-pressure water from the hoses did wash away the gasoline, but since the temperature was very low, the water froze on the concrete almost immediately. Firemen were slipping on the wet ice and falling and swearing.

There was a lot of excitement. Police blocked off the streets around the station. At last, all the gasoline was washed down the storm drains, and it was replaced by thick ice on the platform. The next day a headline in the local paper read, "Truck driver says 'Fill it up' and station owner overdoes it!"

Roger smiled to himself as he pulled into the station with his 1960 Corvette. He had expected to find Ray, but a young boy came out when Roger pulled in. "Where's Ray?" he asked.

"He had an accident and he had to go home to change clothes."

"Did he get hurt?"

"No," the boy laughed. "Ray was doing a tune up on an old car, and since he's short, he had trouble reaching into the engine compartment, so he climbed up on the car and sat with his feet inside next to the engine. When he was finished, he got down and stood looking at his work, and he reached around for a rag in his back pocket, and he could feel only skin. It was his bottom! He had been sitting on the battery, and the small amounts of battery acid on the top of the battery ate through the seat of his pants." He laughed again and went back into the office.

When Roger had finished filling his car with gasoline, he went inside to pay for it. "Nice car, mister," the boy said.

"Thanks." The two talked about early Corvettes for a few minutes. As he walked out toward his car, he saw Em'ly pulling in with her 1955 Corvette.

"Today must be Corvette day at Ray's," he said when she got out of her car.

"The turquoise and copper colors look nice side by side."

"If you had entered the Village show, the two colors could have been side by side. They would reside outside." He forced the silly rhyme because he thought Em'ly would like it.

"Actually, I did send in an entry form for the Village show. As I was getting ready to leave for it, Ben told me that he couldn't come with me. He has been real mean lately. He said that he had to attend to his business— something about reinvesting the funds that

Gordy had left him or he would receive a much lower rate of interest. I had no idea what he was talking about, but I was counting on having him nearby—I just feel safer with him there."

"Because he has a gun?"

She hesitated. "I suppose that's part of the reason."

"The sheriff and I were at the show."

"I didn't know that. After my brother left, I opened a beer as I cleaned my car in the garage. And then another and another. I soon realized that I was in no condition to drive a car, let alone to exhibit one. The decision not to attend the show was made. Actually, I think I was afraid to drive out there alone. So, I sat in my garage and drank some more beer." She was uncharacteristically glum.

"We ought to be able to figure out something to make you feel safe."

Em'ly looked doubtful, but after a moment, she brightened. "I hear that my little sister is working in your office."

"Nell Underwood?"

"Yes."

"I didn't know that you had a younger sister."

"I don't have a biological sister. When I graduated from college, I joined Big Sisters of America. We take younger girls under our wings, mentor them, and point them in the right direction, and Nell became my 'little sister.' She was mixed up with some gang types, but she has straightened herself out. You wouldn't believe how far she has come in a few years."

"I met her only this morning, but she already has impressed me with her initiative. You should have taken her to the car show."

"That's an interesting idea."

As they talked, they saw Ray drive across the platform and park his beloved 1956 Chevy station wagon behind the building. Scowling, he walked around to the front of the station as Roger grinned at him. "Rumor has it that you had an adventure with a battery!"

Ray walked into the office without speaking, and Roger and Em'ly followed. "I hate cars!" Ray said. "And they hate me. Just last week, I had a car on the hoist and a starter I was trying to install slipped and bonked me on the head. That was the same day that a broken hose on the car washing machine soaked me. And look at the scar on this hand—the tire changer ran off the tire rim and did that. Bah. If I had my way, I'd sell this place and open a pizza joint. What's the worst a pizza can do to you? Give you indigestion. You never hear of a pizza destroying the seat of your pants."

"We need a good pizza place in this town," Roger said.

"I will look for you at my grand opening. Do you like pepperoni?"

Roger knew that running a gas station was in Ray's blood and he would never sell it—

although it was a rather ill-fitting occupation for a man who was accident-prone. He was lucky that all of his accidents were relatively minor—and some of them were sources of amusement for his friends.

With a wave to Ray and his young employee, the two Corvette owners sauntered back to their cars. "Let's have an agreement. Any time and any place you want to show your car, let me know, and I will enter that show, and we'll travel to and from it together."

"Why are you so good to me?"

"I want to stay on good terms with your little sister—I need her to organize my office."

"As you suggested, maybe I'll ask Nell if she wants to help me exhibit the car."

"She'd want to put the show cars in the order of the colors of the spectrum."

Em'ly had a blank look on her face.

"She organized my books by color."

CHAPTER 12

J oey tentatively stepped into Roger's garage carrying a six-pack of beer. "I know I'm carrying coals to Newcastle…whatever that means." He opened a beer for himself.

Roger was putting another coat of carnauba wax on his 1960, and he looked up and smiled. "Newcastle Upon Tyne in England was a coal mining center, and didn't need more coal. Open some coal for me, too."

His friend sat on a stool watching Roger. "Are you getting the car ready for another show?"

"No. I am waxing the car as a way of thinking through its restoration. I must decide if I want to keep it as a survivor. Nothing on this car is perfect, but everything is in pretty good condition. Although it was probably due to Brayden's quirky judging, it did win two trophies as a survivor in the Village show."

"I thought Brayden knew a lot about Corvettes."

"Hmmm. That's true."

"I want to ask you about Professor Rebecca Whelk."

"What about her?"

"Didn't you say that she is not a good teacher?"

"Her dean, Keith Jefferson, said something like that before the Promotion and Tenure Committee."

"I am trying to figure out who had a motive to kill Dean Tyler. He was not her dean?"

"No."

"And Tyler had nothing to do with her being denied tenure?"

"I don't know of any connection between the two." Joey didn't seem to have additional questions about the academic world, so Roger continued his thinking about his car. "I want an absolutely first-rate Corvette. I had assumed from the time I purchased this car that I would do a full frame-off restoration to make the car absolutely perfect. Remember, you and I talked about it."

"Yes, I told you that it should be called a 'body-off' restoration."

"I will contact the NCRS and tell them what a grievous blunder they have been making all these years. Anyway, if a full restoration were to be done, should I do it myself? I would like to."

"Can you do it yourself?"

"Probably not. In the first place, I am a full-time professor at the university, and even in the summer, I always teach, and it would therefore take me forever to restore the car in my spare time. And I don't have some of the necessary equipment—I certainly don't have an automotive paint booth or an automobile rotisserie."

"Then you must hire someone to restore the car."

He gulped and said he supposed the decision was obvious. "I will find the best shop I can to do a full frame-off restoration. Thanks for the advice."

Joey laughed, "I'm always glad to share my vast automotive knowledge." He was thoughtful. "You know, we cops sometimes get a hunch. It's nothing based on the facts, but it's something in our bones. I keep connecting Rebecca Whelk and the killing of Dean Tyler—although there's no reason to think that. You told me that she bought a gun, but it's not the caliber of the gun that killed Tyler. And, in any case, you keep telling me that she has no motive."

"Tom Weed told me that Rebecca purchased a .22 from him. You said that Gordy Flowers was killed with a .22."

"Are you suggesting a connection between Whelk and Flowers?"

"No."

"I've seen no evidence that Professor Whelk even knew Gordy Flowers."

"I simply observed that her gun was the same caliber as the one that killed Gordy."

Roger talked with all the Corvette owners he knew about restoration shops. The name of a business in Fergus Falls, Minnesota, was mentioned repeatedly: Pretty Cars, Inc. It was a small shop, but it was experienced in Corvette restoration, and Roger had seen several examples of Pretty Cars' work, and they, indeed, looked pretty. William Prettyman owned the company, and obviously provided its name. Mr. Prettyman did the estimates and paid the bills, but a master Corvette mechanic, Fred Farmer, supervised the restorations. Roger had driven to Minnesota and visited the business and talked at length with both men. The Pretty Cars shop was clean and the tools and equipment were well organized—he knew those were signs of a good shop.

About noon on the first of July, Roger arrived in Fergus Falls with his 1960 in his trailer behind his Hummer. He drove to Pretty Cars, Inc. on the edge of town and unloaded his car and drove it into the Pretty Cars' building. Mr. Prettyman and Fred Farmer shook his hand.

Fred was one of the skinniest men he had ever seen. Roger assumed that he got lots of exercise, both at work and outside his work.

Mr. Prettyman had the extra pounds that Fred did not. He wore a wild Hawaiian shirt with yellow parrots pictured on it, and he looked like a man about to leave on vacation.

He glanced at Roger's car and said, "I'll be right back. I need to get the last car washed out of my system before I look at yours." He went into his office and grabbed a toothbrush and went into the restroom.

Roger gave a questioning look at Fred. "After looking over a car, Mr. Prettyman brushes his teeth before examining another car. He says the practice gives him a clean, fresh look at each vehicle."

Soon, he reappeared, and he and Fred walked slowly around Roger's car.

"Just to be sure we are clear," Mr. Prettyman said, "you want your car to be a historically-accurate NCRS Top-Flight Corvette."

"Exactly."

"You understand that the NCRS judges want Corvettes to meet the standards of vehicle appearance and operation as they were at the time of the car's final assembly—not today's standards. That means that we can't make the car too good; it can't be too shiny or too powerful."

Roger was an unrepentant hot-rodder, and it went against the grain to restore a car with less sparkle and muscle than possible, but he understood that he was entering a different world with early Corvettes. He reluctantly said that he understood.

"Do you like hamburgers?"

"Yes, very much." Roger smiled and lowered his eyebrows in wonder at the question."

"Go to the diner across the street and eat their wonderful hamburgers. By the time you're full, we'll be ready to give you an estimate on the work you want."

"I can do that."

Fred walked with him toward the door. "Since I don't drive a car, I can't go home or downtown for lunch, and I eat at the diner every day, and I recommend their burgers."

"You don't drive a car?"

"Nope. I have a bike that I pedal to the shop."

"You work on cars for a living, but you don't drive?"

"I don't even have a driver's license."

"Really?"

"It's strange, but true." He grinned.

The diner was built in the style that Roger loved: a shining stainless steel train-car shaped building with the scents of French fries and frying burgers hanging over it. A sign declared that the diner featured "Booth Service." Inside, the floors were black and white tile, and the counter and booth seats were pink. Stainless steel surrounded the steaming grill. Roger sat at the counter and was approached by a gum-chewing waitress who asked, "What'll ya have, hon?" He ate three burgers: the double burger with special dressing, an onion ring burger, and a triple burger with cheese. He was full. He was glad to take a short walk down the block prior to crossing the street to Pretty Cars.

When Roger walked back into the shop, Fred was lowering the 1960 from a hoist. "Okay," Mr. Prettyman said, consulting his notes on a clipboard. "We can do a frame-off restoration to transform your great survivor into a perfect Top-Flight Corvette. We can't guarantee how any particular set of NCRS judges will score it, but we will do our best. We estimate that 1200 hours of labor will be required. We will restore the fiberglass body and repaint and reupholster the car. We will replace or re-plate all the chrome and trim. The engine, transmission, and differential will be rebuilt. The car's frame is good, we will simply clean and paint it."

"How long will the restoration take?"

"We can start on the car immediately. Once it's disassembled, Fred will get four teams working on the car simultaneously—one on the fiberglass body, another on the interior, one on the trim, wheels, and frame, and one on the engine, transmission, and differential. Then it will be reassembled. I want to say that it should be finished in two months, by September 1, but check with me during the next few weeks.

Mr. Prettyman showed Roger a total cost figure. It was a large number, but it was actually slightly less than Roger had expected. He nodded and signed the estimate form.

"Just like the hospital, you can see the patient during visiting hours to observe our progress."

"With doctors like you guys, I know that I'm putting my car in good hands."

Roger waved as he walked back to his Hummer. Mr. Prettyman waved back on his way toward the restroom to brush his teeth prior to examining another car.

CHAPTER 13

R oger rarely ate breakfast, and most days, he needed his lunch hour to prepare for his 1:00 class, so he was usually hungry when he returned home at the end of the day. As he walked along the shady sidewalks, he looked up at the mild sun that occasionally poked through the lacy leaves. He thought about food that would be quick to prepare so that he could clean and polish his 2004 for the weekend car show. As soon as he arrived home, he changed into his Saturday clothes.

He would make his own open-face sandwich invention. He placed four slices of white bread on a plate and buttered them. Then he put on American cheese slices, and spread a layer of hotdog mustard over the cheese. Last, he put rings of white onion on top of the mustard. He sat at his table and ate them. The blend of mild cheese, mustard, and raw onion produced a new taste that Roger enjoyed. The sandwiches were so good that he made two more. Then he washed the plate and knife and went out to his garage.

Em'ly wanted to enter her copper '55 in the Classic Corner Car Show on the following weekend, and, as they had agreed, Roger would also enter the show and would accompany her to and from the show and would generally keep an eye on her so that she felt safe. She had said, "Ever since you heard that guy make a rude remark to me and you pounced on the man and pounded him silly, I feel very safe around you." Roger smiled at the memory of the fight—although he knew that he had overdone it. He could better control his anger now.

He was eager to get his 1960 returned to him so that he could show it, but Roger greatly loved showing his 2004. He went over it with clear coat, allowed it to dry, and then polished it with synthetic detail spray. He cleaned the interior and applied leather conditioner to the seats. He put tire gloss on the tires after detailing the chrome wheels. He cleaned and polished the glass and mirrors. He stepped back—the car looked pretty good.

On the bright sunny Saturday morning of the show, he drove his Corvette to Em'ly's home and waited for her in front. When the garage door opened, he saw Nell Underwood walking toward the passenger side of the copper '55. She waved at him, and Em'ly came out a moment later and waved.

The Classic Corner Car Show was sponsored by a convenience store and gas station called the Classic Corner. The large concrete platform was quickly filling with cars when the two Corvettes parked at the end of a long line. Em'ly got out her bag of detailing materials, and demonstrated to Nell how to do a final dusting and polishing of her car. When Roger had finished preparing his 2004, he walked over to the copper '55. "Your car is looking pretty sharp, Em'ly."

"I have a good assistant," she smiled at her little sister.

"I am so glad Em'ly asked me to help," Nell said. "I like being a part in an event with all of these works of modern art."

Under the gentle sun, the three sat in lawn chairs behind Em'ly's Corvette as spectators floated by their cars. From time to time, Roger and Em'ly got up and dusted their cars. Nell watched them and asked, "Why do you guys go to so much trouble to exhibit your wonderful cars? I mean, you take hours and hours preparing them, and you watch over them like your children. Why do you do that?"

"These *are* our children," Roger said.

"As you said earlier, we love art and these cars are works of automotive art that should be exhibited," Em'ly said.

Nell thoughtfully nodded. "I like drama, and I spend hours doing makeup for community theatre productions, so I suppose I have feelings similar to yours—simply over in a different area."

"Exactly," Em'ly said. "Both of my brothers, Ben and Gordy, enjoyed hamming it up in community theatre shows. In fact, they said that you helped them with their makeup when they were in 'Arsenic and Old Lace.'"

"Yes. And I remember that one of my professors acted in that same show—Dr. Whelk. I am not too fond of her as a teacher, but I couldn't believe how good she was playing the part of one of the homicidal spinster aunts. She was very convincing."

All three of them smiled as they remembered the classic farcical black comedy. Nell glanced at Em'ly. "It looked like your brother Ben and Dr. Whelk became close friends as a result of being in that play. At least I saw them off in a corner talking to each other very quietly during rehearsals."

"I didn't realize that my brother even knew her."

"Maybe I'm wrong." Nell looked as if she had let something slip that she should not have mentioned. She shook her head and shrugged her shoulders. "I want to take a closer look at these works of automotive art." She stood up and walked toward the street rods.

Roger and Em'ly watched as Nell approached a '34 Ford rat rod with a large Chrysler engine with a supercharger bulging from the front end. She exchanged a few words with the car's owner—a rather greasy young man. After giving him a friendly smile, she walked on.

Em'ly looked as if she were glad that Nell's absence gave her an opportunity to talk to

Dr. Strong. "Do you know how the sheriff is progressing with his investigation of my brother Gordy's murder?"

"I have talked with him. He…ah…has several lines of investigation in mind."

Em'ly gave a short humorless laugh. "You mean he has no idea who shot Gordy."

"I am afraid that's correct." He smiled slightly. "You can see right through me."

"He was a good brother, and he deserves better. Not to mention that his killer shouldn't be roaming around out there."

"The sheriff is clever and tireless, and it may take time, but he will catch the person who committed this crime."

"You're sure?"

"Yes. The mills of the gods grind slowly, but they grind exceedingly fine."

"I hope you're right."

"I know that I'm right. Like us, the sheriff does not approve of murder."

Em'ly nodded, and she and Roger sat in silence.

When Nell returned she was grinning. "I found Christine!"

"Is she one of your friends?"

"No, no, no. I mean I found Christine from the Stephen King novel and the movie!"

While Roger looked blank, Em'ly understood at once. "You discovered a red 1958 Plymouth Fury." She had once shown a PT Cruiser, and she knew more about Plymouths than Roger—also, she was more in tune with the culture that had spun a cult surrounding the malevolent car from the horror film. There was even an International Christine Club. She and Nell left Roger to watch over the Corvettes and they went to look at Christine.

When Em'ly returned, she told Dr. Strong, "It was 'Christine,' alright! We stood and stared at her—waiting for her to do something evil, but the car simply sat there.

Nell is fascinated with the car, and she is still talking to its owner. It is indeed a red 1958 Plymouth Fury, but it had to be repainted red since that color was not really used on a Fury in 1958. I preferred the strictly original 1957 Fury that was next to Christine. The Sand Dune White paint with the unique gold side trim and grille is striking."

The two Corvette owners sat silent for a few minutes. Roger could see Darrell Yorick's Commemorative Edition Corvette in the distance, and it brought Em'ly's earlier remarks to his mind. "When we first talked about your brother's killing, you suspected that it could have been done by someone who was envious of his Corvette."

"I still think that."

"I see Darrell Yorick over there…"

"Where?"

"Half way up the second row." Em'ly did not immediately spot him. "He's wearing a green shirt," Roger said.

"Oh … yeah, I see him next to his white car."

"Do you suspect him?"

Their conversation was interrupted by the announcement of awards. All of the exhibitors shuffled toward the front of the convenience store where the public address system was located. Roger won a trophy for the best paint—he assumed that it was a trophy for the brightest paint. When Em'ly won first place in the Corvette division, Nell was much more excited about the honor than Em'ly. Darrell Yorick won a trophy for the best sports car. He looked very satisfied. The last trophy to be awarded was for the best car in the show, and it was also awarded to Yorick. He was clearly delighted, and he looked from side to side as he walked forward to accept the trophy—his appearance was that of a man who had at last received justice.

As they were packing up, both Em'ly and Roger looked toward Yorick. He was grinning and telling anyone who was nearby about

ERIC JOHNSON

his unique car. Roger said, "You were about to tell me if you suspected that Yorick had something to do with your brother's death."

"You have heard him ranting about not winning as much as he thinks he deserves. Do you think that kind of attitude can turn bitter and violent?"

"I suppose so, but I don't know much about criminal psychology."

"Yorick's bank worked with Gordy's investment company to issue some financial bonds or stocks, and I saw him at Gordy's house, and I later talked with him at a party that my brother hosted to celebrate their agreement. He was nice enough at the party. He always seemed nice—except when he was talking about showing his car."

"Can you tell me more about the financial business that Yorick and your brother worked on?"

She shook her head. "No. I understand nothing about business. I wouldn't recognize a stock or bond if it walked up to me." She was silent a moment. "But I do understand this:—just as Stephen King's Christine was evil, so there are things in this world that are evil, and they cost poor Gordy his life."

CHAPTER 14

Professor Roger Strong was the first to admit—in fact, to insist—that he was an amateur who enjoyed puttering with cars, but he was a professional when it came to his teaching. He wanted to impart knowledge of great literature to his students, but more important, he wanted them to enjoy and appreciate the classics.

He occasionally found the need to lecture to his classes. Students usually didn't like lectures, and, even when Roger made them as entertaining as he could, students tended to tune them out, but the traditional lecture was still the fastest, most efficient method of imparting information. As his Introduction to Literature class was starting a new unit on poetry, he needed to summarize common poetic practices. He considered how best to retain the attention of his students. When he was in his teens, Roger was interested in juggling and other circus skills. He still had a bag full of equipment. He wondered if doing circus tricks during his lecture would effectively keep the students focused.

He entered the classroom with a large burlap bag and put it down with a clunk next to the podium. He quickly checked attendance, and then took a bright yellow juggling club from the bag. Without any explanation, he tossed the club into the air and caught it after it had revolved one full turn, and he said, "It is important to notice poetic meter. It is composed of a regular pattern of stressed and unstressed syllables." As he described increasingly complex meters, he added one brightly-colored club after another to his juggling. When he was keeping five clubs in the air, he said, "Iambic pentameter, with five feet, is the most common meter in English." He caught the five clubs and put them back in the bag. "Rhythm is a simple form of pleasure, and it's helpful to notice it," he said.

"Now, poetry commonly uses what are called figures of speech. The metaphor (along with its cousin the simile) and symbolism are the most important figures of speech." He pulled a shining chrome unicycle from the bag, and he hopped on it and rode it unsteadily around the podium as he described how metaphors work. He gave examples and made one revolution for each example.

"Now the simile is like a metaphor, but it travels in a little different direction to get to the same point." He peddled the unicycle backwards around the podium and talked about how a simile explained the basis of the comparison. "Almost always the words 'like' or 'as' are used in a simile."

As Roger was about to move to another topic, a student asked a question. "Professor, if I say, 'my house is like your house,' is that a simile?"

"Excellent question. The answer is, no, 'my house is like your house' is not a simile. When a simile is used, we must be able to identify the subject being described and the vehicle being used to describe it. Consider this sentence—'Bill is as clumsy as an elephant.' It is obvious that we are talking about Bill, he is the subject, and we bring in the elephant simply as a vehicle to describe how clumsy he is. Now, if we say, 'my house is like your house,' we can't tell which is which. Okay?"

The student nodded.

"Also, both a metaphor and a simile compare things that are essentially different, unlike the comparison of houses."

The student nodded again.

Roger was getting tired of riding the unicycle, but he wanted to finish his answer while on it. "Another difference is that the sentence about the houses does not spell out the basis of the comparison. If I say, 'my house is as dirty as a dump,' that would be a simile since the basis of the comparison is the dirt and garbage in a dump which is mentioned to describe the house."

The student tipped his head to indicate that he was well satisfied. Roger could have said more, but his butt was getting sore, so he stopped and put the unicycle down.

"Symbolism is more complicated," he said. He took a coil of clothesline wire from the bag and pulled it straight across the room. "I should stretch this wire between two buildings downtown, about 200 feet from the ground, and walk on the wire between the buildings." He stood on the wire on the floor. "However, I'll explain symbolism here in the classroom because you might not be able to hear me if I were 200 feet in the air." He described symbolism and gave a series of examples as he carefully put one foot in front of the other and slowly walked on the wire across the room, with a good deal of hesitation and a few backward steps to keep his balance. When he safely reached the far side of the room, he turned and bowed deep from the waist. The room erupted with applause. "Thank you. Thank you. You are too kind," he said.

As students were leaving and Roger was packing up his circus supplies and his books, he reflected that class discussion was effective, and it certainly was easier for him than a circus performance. When he walked into the hallway he could hear raised voices in the seminar room.

He knew that there had been a meeting of the Curriculum Committee in the seminar room the preceding hour during his class, but the meeting should have been over by the time his class was finished. He glanced into the seminar room. Two professors, Dr.

Rebecca Whelk and Dr. Susan Mendenhall, stood toe to toe. Both were red in the face and their hands at their sides were clenched into fists.

Roger didn't know if he should quickly walk away and pretend he had seen nothing, or if he should intrude and try to make peace. The decision was made for him when both women turned and looked directly at him.

"Let's ask Roger," Rebecca said.

"Yes. He will know," Susan said.

Roger wished he had walked away, but now he had no choice but to step forward. "How can I help?"

Rebecca Whelk sneered as she spoke. "Everyone but the most ignorant would know that a motion to table something is not debatable, exactly like a motion to adjourn. Isn't that right?"

Before Roger had a chance to say anything, Susan Mendenhall moved forward and pushed Rebecca to the side. "No, that is not correct. The only motion that is not debatable is the motion to adjourn. In any case, the committee did adjourn, so there is nothing to debate. Rebecca doesn't need to be so disagreeable over a parliamentary rule."

"If I'm being disagreeable, you're dishonest!"

"I'm being responsible."

"You're obtuse and slow-witted. And you're not honest. I don't believe what you told me about Darrell Yorick. He is a kind and caring man."

"Roger, say something."

Both professors stared at him. "Okay, perhaps I can be of help with parliamentary procedure, but, first, both of you take a deep breath and take a step back." When they had done that, he continued. "Rebecca, as a factual matter, *Robert's Rules of Order* states that a motion to adjourn is a privileged motion (and thus not debatable), but a motion to table something is not in that category."

Rebecca looked very offended. "You just made that up!" She brushed past Roger and looked back. "Susan, you have not heard the last of this! And the next time Darrell asks me to go to dinner, I am going to accept!" She quickly strode off toward her office.

Susan looked grimly at Roger. "Sometimes I think I could kill that woman," she said. "This was supposed to be a routine meeting to approve courses to be offered next summer, and Rebecca made a battle zone out of it."

"What was that about Darrell Yorick?"

"Oh, I thought I was doing Rebecca a favor. I happened to talk to Darrell at a party, and he asked me if he would have any chance to date her. I didn't encourage him to ask her out, and I wanted to change the subject, but he pursued his question, and I had to say that I did not think that she would accept. I simply told her that, and she acted as if I was accusing him of something or defaming him."

"And that's why she defended him?"

"I guess so, but she was simply angry about the tabled motion. She doesn't care about Darrell." As Susan quickly walked away, she warily looked toward Rebecca's office as if the angry professor might suddenly emerge and attack her.

Roger returned to his office and sat at his desk remembering what he had just seen and heard. "The reason that academic disputes are so bitter is that the stakes are so low," he said to himself. "And how many times have I said that?" But, he thought, there was something almost pathological about Rebecca's anger. He remember Mr. Weed's regret that he had sold her a gun.

Nell Underwood tapped at the door and then tentatively entered. "Good morning, Dr. Strong."

"Hi, Nell." He remembered that she was scheduled to work for two hours that morning. She sat in front of the computer assuming that he would have work for her to enter on it.

"I see that you have recovered from the hard work of helping Em'ly polish her car at the show this weekend."

"Oh, that was fun—it was not like work at all. I loved seeing all the great cars—especially Christine!"

"Would you like to own a car like Christine?"

"No!" She looked shocked. "It was fun to see, but I wouldn't want an evil car in my garage. Some day I'd like a car exactly like your yellow convertible."

"When you spend all day with Em'ly and me at a car show, what does your boyfriend say?"

"Oh, I don't have a boyfriend."

"Really?" Nell was such an attractive young woman that Roger had expected that she had multiple boyfriends.

"For years I had one boyfriend after another, and they always got caught robbing a store or stealing a car or committing some other crime, and they always went to jail. One of my girlfriends once told me that I had more ex-boyfriends in the slammer than most girls have their whole lives."

"Really?" He grinned, but he quickly wiped the grin off his face as he realized that Nell was sadly serious.

"I think I simply have a way of picking losers. So now I don't have a special boyfriend, but I try to be nice to everyone."

Roger wondered if that attitude accounted for her flirting with so many boys. He gave Nell several bibliographies and class outlines that he needed updated and put on web pages for future classes that he would teach. She needed to move the burlap bag to make room to sit at the computer, and as she did that, one of the juggling clubs rolled out. She looked at it with mild wonder.

Roger answered her unasked question by digging into the bag and withdrawing several additional clubs, and stood in front of her juggling them rapidly. "I brought these to my literature class today to provide entertainment while I lectured about deadly boring topics."

"Oh, Dr. Strong, you are the cleverest professor on campus. I sure wish I had taken your literature class rather than the one I took from Dr. Whelk."

He smiled and made no comment. *It's nice to receive a compliment* he thought.

When he arrived home, Roger changed clothes, ate a sandwich, and went out to his garage. He turned on the TV and tuned it to the football channel and found a repeated broadcast of an interesting game from the previous season. The weather for the game was cold with rain changing to snow, and the players slipped and slid around on the field. When Roger had played football, he had always wanted a nice day for a game—a crisp fall day was ideal. He hated to play in the snow and cold. However, he loved watching football games on TV that were played in bad weather—the worse the weather, the more enjoyable to watch. Perhaps he liked the contrast between the snug warm room where he sat with a TV set and the nasty weather on the field.

With one eye on the TV set, Roger put the top down on his Corvette and prepared to put leather conditioner on the seats. He took out several well-washed towels and a bottle of conditioner. He put a small amount of the liquid conditioner on a folded towel and rubbed it on the top of one seat and then worked it in with a soft brush.

He looked up to see Joey standing in the center of the side door. Pretty much filling the doorway, the sheriff stood watching Roger for a moment and then said, "I thought you would want someone to show you the right way to put on that stuff!"

"I would be eternally grateful for any crumbs of knowledge you could condescend to offer me."

"It will cost you."

"I'll pay you with cold liquid refreshments from my refrigerator."

"That's what I had in mind."

Joey squirted the conditioner directly on the leather seat and then rubbed it around before he worked it in with the brush.

"By watching you, I have learned something already. You put the stuff on the seat rather than on a towel so that you will make the process more difficult for yourself and thus you give yourself more beneficial exercise."

Joey looked a little surprised that he had made a mistake in a process that appeared so simple. He continued with the joking banter, "I didn't want to show you too many of my secrets all at once, but since you already know that it's best to put the conditioner on the towel, I'll do it that way."

The sweet scents of leather floated up toward the men and soon completely filled the garage. When they had buffed the leather with clean towels, they tossed them into a bin.

Roger looked serious. "Today I accidentally witnessed a fight between two professors. It was about a trivial matter, but it was about as bitter as any I have seen in academia. The conclusion was that Susan Mendenhall said she would like to kill Rebecca Whelk."

It was obvious that the statement registered with the sheriff, but he did not reply.

CHAPTER 15

lthough Roger's 1960 had been at Pretty Cars only a little over two weeks, he was eager to see how Fred Farmer and his crew were progressing with it. He enjoyed the drive to Fergus Falls early in the day, and he arrived about mid-morning.

When Roger walked into the shop, the first sight that greeted him was the bare chassis of his car. It was rather shocking to see the bare frame and differential with no body or engine. It looked naked and embarrassed. He didn't see his engine or transmission, but off to one side, the car's fiberglass body was mounted on a large rotisserie that had been rotated to put the body at a rather drunken angle. The turquoise paint was completely removed from the body, and it had blotchy shades of gray, yellow, and white. Most alarming were the cracks in the body, and there were small gaps where pieces of fiberglass were missing.

Mr. Prettyman emerged from his office and greeted him. "Ah, Roger, you are here to visit the patient. She is doing as well as could be expected."

"You've done a lot since I left the car."

"Yup. I told you it would be finished by September 1, and we intend to keep our word." Mr. Prettyman walked over to the coffee machine and returned with a cup filled with black coffee for Roger—he didn't bother to ask how he took his coffee, or even if he liked coffee. In a garage, you drink black coffee— it's considered sissy to add sugar or cream.

"Fred, can you join us?"

Fred Farmer left a group of men who were gathered around the rear of the body of Roger's car and stood with his boss and Roger.

"Describe our progress to Roger."

"As you can see, we've disassembled your car. We're working on the body—more about it in a moment. The engine and transmission have all the correct numbers and dates, and they're being cleaned and rebuilt. The frame is in excellent condition—it has superficial surface rust but it isn't damaged or pitted. Even the cross members are in good condition. We will clean and paint the frame."

Mr. Prettyman looked on proudly as Fred spoke as if to signify that this was his man and he was sticking by him.

"Our only real concerns are with the body. We'd like to know what you want done about a few things." The three men walked toward the body on the automotive rotisserie. Close up, the body of Roger's Corvette looked even shabbier.

"We don't think your car has ever been in a collision—that's the good news. However, you can see that there are a number of stress cracks, and in some spots the cracks are close together and small sections of fiberglass are crumbling."

Roger nodded. He had no idea that under the quiet, pastel paint there would be such a mess.

"I'm sure you know that a Corvette is not one large fiberglass casting but is rather assembled from quite a few panels that are bonded together. Now, we are getting to my question. Notice the crack in the fender here. We have three options. First, we could try to repair the crack. Second, we could replace the fender panel with a panel from an after-market supplier. Third, we could replace the panel with a good used part from a car of the same year. What do you want us to do?"

"What do you recommend?"

"Since you want your Corvette to be exactly like it rolled off the assembly line, I strongly recommend replacing panels, not repairing them. We will try to find good panels in Corvette salvage yards, that's best, but it's also the most expensive. We should be able to find good rear panels, since cars are less likely to suffer accident damage in the back end. For the front, we may have to order them from an after-market supplier. We will make sure that supplier sends us fiberglass that has been press molded so that it's smooth on both sides."

"Replacing the panels with the originals from other cars, if possible, is what I want."

"Good. There's something you should know about replacing panels. We will make sure that the joints are secure and that the bonding strips are in the same places as manufactured. However, assuming you want this, we'll be messy with the adhesive on the bonding strips on the inside of the body—we will allow it to harden as it drips from the strips and oozes from the joints. That is the way the cars were originally made—after all, the outside of the panels is what is seen and that was what was important to the guys at the plant."

"That kind of thing makes me uneasy, but if that's the way it was done, so be it."

"Ask Roger about the paint," Mr. Prettyman said.

"Will the color be different?"

"No, no. We have the codes for 1960 Corvette Tasco Turquoise paint, and we can get the color perfect. The color is not the problem. The issues are with the kind of paint and its appearance. The car was originally painted with DuPont Lucite acrylic lacquer, and its production was discontinued years ago. The stock on hand was even recalled from distributors. Do you want me to use lacquer if we can find it?"

"Isn't acrylic lacquer dangerous stuff that is illegal in some states?"

"Yes," Mr. Prettyman said.

"What's the alternative?"

Fred looked as if he expected that question. "Use a modern polyurethane base coat/clear coat paint, but don't apply the clear coat. I can spray the base coat so that it looks like lacquer."

"What's the disadvantage of doing that?"

"Well, the paint will not have the reflective qualities and wet look of base coat/clear coat, but it will have a nice deep glow—very much like the appearance of acrylic lacquer. A disadvantage for some people is that the absence of a clear coat will make the paint less durable, but I assume that you're not going to leave the car out in the weather— it'll be garaged when you are not driving it or showing it?"

"Yes, of course. Okay. Do what you said— paint the car with polyurethane base coat without the clear coat."

"There is one last related paint question. The NCRS dictates deductions for over restoration. Some amount of orange peel in the paint is expected—not a lot, but some—say, a bit of bumpy stuff on the bottoms of the doors. I can hold the paint gun farther away in those places so that the thinner evaporates before the paint hits, and that will produce orange peel. Do you want a little of that?"

"Wow, that is a philosophical question. Should a car deliberately and obviously be restored to look worse than it would have to look? As a car guy, this really runs against the grain." Roger paced a few steps from the men as he considered the issue.

"It's your decision. We can easily paint it with or without obvious orange peel," Mr. Prettyman said. "Why don't you go across the street and have a juicy triple burger and think about the question and come back and tell us what you want."

Roger had to eat two triple burgers (with a large order of onion rings) in order to think through the issue. He had been asked to make three concessions in order to make a typical 1960 Corvette. First, he agreed that the underside of the panel joints could look like sloppy joes. Well, that was not a big deal since only a judge peering under the car could see them. Second, he had agreed to use a modern paint that would appear to be the same as the factory paint. That was okay. But did he want the paint to have some fine bumps in the surface? The original cars always had some orange peel.

As he finished his second burger, he made up his mind. He paid for his food and quickly walked across the street to Pretty Cars.

"Well?" Mr. Prettyman asked as Roger came striding into the shop. They both walked back to the car's body where Fred was working with his men. All of them stood waiting for the big decision.

"Consistent with the appearance of acrylic lacquer, the paint should be as free of obvious orange peel as possible—except in one obscure spot—say across one panel under the rear bumper. I want it both ways—anyone who looks at the car, and even examines it fairly close, should not spot any significant orange peel, but if a judge says, 'Hold on, this car is over restored,' I can point to the paint under the bumper."

Both Mr. Prettyman and Fred smiled, nodded, and agreed with Roger's decision. They acted as if the question of painting a Corvette was a very difficult game, and Roger had triumphed in winning it in a very clever way, and they were glad for him.

That night, Joey and Roger sat in his garage with a Cubs baseball game on the TV in the background. Since neither man had ever lived in Chicago, it was difficult to explain their impassioned loyalty to the Cubs, but they were adamant. Roger explained in detail how he had made a series of tough decisions about his 1960 earlier that day—in particular, he explained the differences between the DuPont Lucite acrylic lacquer used in 1960 and modern polyurethane base coat/clear coat paint. Joey shook his head and said, "Too much information."

"Then let's talk about something else. You wondered if Yorick had any business dealings with Gordy Flowers. Em'ly and I entered the Classic Corner show last Sunday, and she told me that Yorick's bank issued stock or bonds to raise money for Gordy's investment company. Apparently it was a big deal because they had a party at Gordy's house to celebrate the transaction."

"That's interesting. Yorick dislikes Gordy because his car wins more awards, but he works with him in business."

"Perhaps it was simply a mutually beneficial financial deal."

"I'm not sure. Rumor has it that Gordy was making risky investments in unsecured bundled loans, and when they failed, the bank was left holding the bag. To make matters worse, Ben has been lazy about running the business that Gordy left him and has made some stupid decisions, and he and his banker stand to lose a vast amount of money. I assume from what you just told me that Yorick is the banker."

"So now Yorick has a reason to hold a grudge against the younger brother too."

CHAPTER 16

n his office, Roger sat at his desk re-reading a novel that he had assigned to his nineteenth-century literature class. Nell Underwood was busily working at his office computer—typing a syllabus for a humanities class that Roger would teach the following semester. Once in a while when she would mistype something, she would show that she was peeved by quietly uttering a four-letter word. She had just finished listing the required textbooks for the course when her face brightened.

"I think I would like this book," she said.

Since Nell was still in her teens and had run with a rough group of friends, he was a little surprised that she would be attracted to books about classical music, art, and literature. He looked over her shoulder to see the title of the book: *A History of Western Music*. He was puzzled a moment until he realized that Nell assumed that the text was about country-western music. He said simply, "If you enrolled in the course, you would find that there are several kinds of 'western' music."

Rebecca Whelk came striding into his office through the open door. Without preface she asked, "Do you have a red pen that I could borrow? The papers that I'm correcting are so bad that I've used up all my red pens, and I don't have time to get more from the bookstore right now."

Roger took a pen out of his desk and handed it to Rebecca. "Is one enough?"

"Yes, I'm almost done." She didn't seem to notice his mild sarcasm. "Say, you have a new bookcase! How do you rate?"

"I simply asked to use one that was stored in the business school."

"And look at the goofy way you have your books arranged." She laughed. "Are they in some kind of order based on color?"

"Yes. Nell organized them for me, and I love the system."

"Well, it's not very intellectual—in fact, it's stupid! You should put books with similar content together."

"They're my books, and I prefer them like this."

Rebecca turned on her heel, and strode out of the office.

It was very quiet in the office for a few minutes, and then Nell said, "I'm sorry if I did something wrong."

"No, you didn't. I like what you did. You were very clever. Dr. Whelk simply has different ideas about books." He gave Nell another syllabus to type, and at once she was clacking away on it, but Roger noticed that she didn't look very happy.

"I have to run down to the college office," Roger said. "I'll be back in a few minutes." Instead of going to the college office, he headed directly for Rebecca Whelk's office. He knew he had to keep his anger under control. He would be polite, but he would make his point. He quietly knocked on the closed door and was told to enter.

"Good morning, again, Rebecca." She didn't immediately look up from her papers. He closed the door behind him and waited in silence. When she did look at him, he asked, "Did you have to be so critical about the order of my books?"

"As I said, they look goofy."

"How they look is not the point. Little Nell was proud of her work, and I liked it, and now you have hurt her feelings."

"And now I must watch out for the feelings of your flirt of an office assistant? She is only a student."

"I don't know that she's a flirt, and, in any case, you should respect the feelings of everyone."

"Yeah, like Dean Jefferson respected my feelings by denying me tenure."

"This has nothing to do with your tenure."

"Sure, right."

Roger had vowed not to get angry, but he could feel dark clouds of emotion swelling within him. He knew he had to leave. Could he say something polite as he exited? He turned to open the office door, and he saw Rebecca's pink coat and a yellow scarf hanging from a coat hook on the back of the door. "I like your bright clothing!" Rebecca had looked down at her papers again and didn't answer.

When Roger had asked his bank to transfer the money to purchase the 1960 from Tom Weed, he had depleted his checking account and needed to transfer something from his savings to pay his living expenses until his next payday. During an open hour of the early afternoon, Roger drove downtown. He loved the old bank building with its high ceilings and marble columns. As soon as he had walked into the bank, he spotted the bank officer that he usually dealt with, but there were two men waiting to see him. Roger took a chair next to them and looked out the window. Almost immediately, he heard his name.

"Roger, do you need help?" It was Darrell Yorick who had come out of his office. He noticed that Yorick was wearing a green shirt with a web pattern of fine black lines, and it looked like printed money—that must be the reason that he always wore that shirt on working days.

"Hi, Darrell. I simply wanted some advice about cashing in a CD."

"Come back to my office. I can help you."

"Okay." Roger was surprised, but as he walked to the president's office, he supposed that Yorick was adopting a hands-on-CEO type of practice that had become popular in some businesses.

Yorick thoughtfully listened to Roger's description of his finances, and he suggested that Roger keep his CD to maturity and borrow against it for immediate needs. He could give Roger a short-term loan at a lower rate of interest than the CD was earning, and thus everyone would come out ahead. An assistant prepared the necessary forms while Roger and Yorick waited.

Yorick leaned back in his large desk chair. "As I'm sure you know, I worked with your colleague, Dean Tyler, and I was very sorry to hear of his death. He was a member of our bank advisory board, and he and I were co-chairs of the city Red Cross fund drive. I really regret that he and I had that blow-out argument."

Apparently Yorick was under the impression that the university faculty and deans were members of a close family and that they all understood the affairs of one another. Roger had no idea that Dean Tyler knew Yorick, much less that they had had an argument.

"He is going to be sadly missed," Roger mumbled. He didn't know what else to say. Of course it was a tragedy that a dean was killed, but the faculty in Arts and Sciences were only vaguely aware of the dean of the Business School.

Yorick sat forward. "Are you going to enter the Canton show next weekend?"

"Yes. How about you?"

"I'm considering it."

Roger knew that Yorick was passionate about showing his 53/03 Corvette, and, despite his seeming reluctance, Yorick was sure to exhibit in the large Canton show.

On a beautiful late afternoon at the end of summer, Roger and Joey sat on an old leather couch in Roger's garage, and the two men stared out the open garage door as they talked. "I shouldn't tell tales out of school," Roger said, "But Rebecca Whelk really made me angry yesterday. My office assistant, Nell Underwood, arranged my books in order of color—they look like a rainbow, and I like it a lot. Well, Whelk came striding into my office in her usual impudent way, and she said the arrangement of books was stupid. Nell was sitting right there and heard her, and she was simply crushed. If Nell were still running with her rough friends, Whelk would have flat tires on her car."

Joey nodded, but he didn't seem eager to learn details about the academic world.

"You'll be more interested in something else that I learned. Darrell Yorick had some kind of fight with Milton Tyler."

"I didn't know they were acquainted."

"When I was in the bank, he told me that the two of them served on committees, and he assumed that I knew that he and Tyler had had some kind of blowout argument, and he said he now regretted it."

"This is indeed interesting. So Yorick had a grudge against two men, and both of them were killed. First, Gordy's car was beating Yorick's car, and he resented it, and there are questions about their business relationship. Second, Yorick had an argument with Dean Tyler."

"That's true, but if you're thinking that Yorick might have shot both Gordy and Tyler, why would he have used a different caliber gun for each of them?"

"I don't know. I'm simply reciting facts."

CHAPTER 17

Roger looked up at the sky as he tentatively stepped out of his house. The dark clouds hung low and rain threatened. The air was warm and heavy. He hurriedly walked toward school, hoping to arrive before he got wet. He was the chair of the Buildings and Grounds Committee, and a vote needed to be taken on the question of whether to recommend building an addition to the Business School. Rebecca Whelk was a member of the committee, and he knew that she strongly opposed the addition. As expected, the business faculty would champion the addition, and therefore, this would probably be a heated meeting.

At the end of the hallway, Nell Underwood was pacing back and forth near his office. She apparently was waiting for Roger to unlock the office and assign her some tasks. As he fumbled with his keys, she shifted her weight from foot to foot—she seemed eager to get into the office. He was surprised that she had arrived an hour earlier than he had expected. Apparently she wanted to do well in her new job. When they were in the office, he put the books he carried on his desk and found the folder for his meeting. He handed Nell a bibliography that he had annotated by hand and asked that it be entered on his computer and added to the website for a class, and then he rushed off to his meeting.

The seminar room in the business building was not air conditioned, and it was so humid that the air felt almost liquid. Roger was the first to arrive, and he put his folder on the end of the long table and paged through the papers as he sat waiting for the other committee members. When the 8:00 a.m. scheduled starting time for the meeting arrived, they started to stumble into the room. Most of the faculty members murmured excuses that they would never accept from tardy students. When it was 8:15, all of the ten members were assembled except for Prof. Whelk. Roger decided to delay the start of the meeting a little longer. When she had not arrived at 8:30, he called the meeting to order.

As the Acting Dean of the Business School, Dr. Susan Mendenhall made a highly statistical presentation arguing the need for significantly more square footage for the business programs. She was as polite and charming as Roger had ever seen her. She related a funny story about students sitting on window ledges that illustrated the crowded conditions. Several faculty members asked questions about the cost of the addition, and

Susan had specific answers at her fingertips. She argued that it was to the benefit of the whole university to build an addition to the business building since it would require fewer business classes scheduled in other campus buildings.

More quickly than Roger had imagined possible, the committee was ready for a vote. The motion to support the construction of an addition to the business building was carried by an apparently unanimous voice vote. He looked around to see if anyone wanted to ask for a countable vote, such as a show of hands. Apparently everyone was content with the voice vote. Since there was no further business on the agenda, the meeting was adjourned.

The faculty members dispersed far more quickly than they had assembled. Susan Mendenhall took her time gathering her papers and then walked over to Roger. "You chaired a very good meeting, Roger. Thank you."

ERIC JOHNSON

"I simply kept us on task. You made a very persuasive presentation, and the natural consequence was a favorable vote. *You* are the person to be complimented."

"Well, thank you, but I think we both know that the absence of one committee member made the meeting run smoother and insured that the motion would pass."

Roger acknowledged the observation with a slight smile and a nod as Susan left the room. Standing alone in the conference room, he wondered why Rebecca had missed the meeting. On his way back to his building, he mused that missing a meeting that promised a fierce fight was not Rebecca's style. As he reached the hallway near his office, he turned toward her office. He stopped at her door and knocked. He heard only silence. He knocked again. Nothing. Without thinking, he tried the door as he was about to turn away, and the door opened—it was not locked. "Rebecca," he called as he peered in.

Dr. Whelk was lying on the floor in front of her desk. Roger quickly ran to her side, and he felt for a pulse in her neck but could not detect any. And her skin was cool to the touch. There was a brownish-red patch that looked like blood on the side of her head. As he pulled back, he noticed a small .22 caliber automatic near her outstretched hand on top of papers sliding out of a folder labeled "Buildings and Grounds Committee." He stepped away and backed out the door and closed it. He sprinted to his office and called 911.

"A woman in the Arts and Sciences Office Building at the university appears to be dead. Please send an ambulance and the police. They should come to the second floor, and I'll wait in the hallway and direct them to the correct office."

He listened for a moment. "Yes, the Arts and Sciences Office Building—second floor."

Nell stopped typing and stared with a horrified look at the rapidly moving professor. "What happened?" she asked.

"Professor Whelk has been… killed. Or, I guess… I suppose… she killed herself—in her office. I found her."

"Should I leave?"

"Ah, probably not. Just sit tight. Keep the door closed—in fact, it might be wise to keep it locked." He went back into the hallway after locking the door behind him and waited for the EMTs to arrive.

The next few hours were a blur. Roger heard sirens outside his building, and when the EMTs rushed up the stairs, he simply said, "Room 210," and pointed toward Whelk's office, and they tumbled off in that direction. Police arrived including Sheriff Joey Bucket. He quietly asked to talk with Roger in an empty classroom, and the two of them sat in student desks and closed the door.

"I understand that you found the body?"

"Yes."

"Briefly, but completely, I want you to tell me how you discovered Professor Whelk."

"I knocked on her door.... But wait, let me back up. Rebecca failed to attend a meeting in the business building first thing this morning. I thought that with her strong opinions...but never mind that now. It simply was strange that she would miss the meeting, and I knocked on her door when I returned to this building after the meeting. There was no answer, and I opened the door and saw her on the floor." Roger paused.

"Take your time," Joey said. "Did you know immediately that she was dead?"

"I checked for a pulse, and when I found none, I left and called 911 from my office."

Joey was taking notes. "Did you touch anything?"

"I don't think so. Only the door and her neck when I checked for a pulse. Of course I've been in that office dozens of times—

including just the other day when I chastised her for insulting Nell's book arrangements."

Joey nodded. "Of course."

"And I saw a small gun on the floor next to Rebecca."

"Had you ever seen that gun before?"

"No."

"You were in the business building with other faculty until just before you went to Professor's Whelk's office?

"Yes."

"Were there other people on the second floor during your meeting? They might have noticed something."

"My office assistant, Nell Underwood, was working in my office."

"I'll want to talk to her."

As Sheriff Bucket talked with Nell in his office, Roger stood staring out the window in the hallway. The sky was even darker than it had been when Roger arrived, and rain was starting to fall. It looked as if it could rain all day. The sheriff emerged with Nell, and Roger told her to go home—they wouldn't do any more work that day. All classes in the building were cancelled. Roger thought he would go home himself.

In his rush to get to his early meeting, Roger had neglected to bring a raincoat to the university, but he had an umbrella in his office. It was a pastel green—the only color available for sale in the bookstore when he needed to buy an umbrella. It kept him dry, but Roger considered the color rather sissy, and a fellow faculty member had said to him, "You must be really confident of your masculinity to carry that color umbrella!"

Roger found walking in the rain a pleasurable, calming experience. The world around him was muted in the mist. The water seemed to drop straight down from the dark gray skies. The sounds of the rain on the umbrella and on the sidewalk were comforting.

When Roger approached his house, he was surprised to see his neighbor, Mr. Bickett, mowing his lawn in the rain, and Roger stopped and watched him. The small engine on the lawn mower was roaring at high speed and large clumps of wet grass were flying out in every direction from under the mower. When the blade of the mower collided with clumps of sticky grass that built up under the mower, there was a rumpty-tumpty sound as the clumps broke up and flew out.

Mr. Bickett was glancing up at the clouds and whistling as he passed back and forth across his yard. He was enjoying his mowing. When he spotted Roger, he stopped and shut off the mower. "Hey, neighbor," he said.

"Hey. I've never seen anyone mow his lawn in the rain before."

"Oh? Well, it was common for us to do that at the end of the summer on the farm. My father always said that if we cut the grass in the rain, the soil is stimulated, and it will spread to the trees, and they will change color sooner and the fall season will arrive sooner."

"Really?"

"I've never seen it fail."

"It's been a hot, humid summer, and I'm ready for an end to this summer."

"So am I. That's why I decided to mow when I saw it raining. Hey, what happened over at your school this morning? I was in my garage in the alley, and I can see your college building down the alley. There were all kinds of police and rescue trucks with lights flashing."

"A faculty member apparently shot herself. I discovered the body."

"Oh, good grief. That's terrible. That makes two shootings recently. What's going on over there?"

"I don't know."

"When I saw people going in the building early this morning, I had no idea."

"Who did you see?"

"I don't know their names, of course, but there was a young girl, a woman wearing a pink coat, a man in a green shirt, and you."

Roger reflected. The girl would be Nell arriving early to work, and the woman in pink would be Rebecca Whelk. Who was the man in green? Could it have been Yorick? He often wore a green shirt, but certainly many others might have had on a green shirt.

"I'd better finish the lawn before the mower gets so wet that it won't start." Mr. Bickett waved as he walked back to his machine, and soon it was roaring again, and clumps of wet grass were flying everywhere.

CHAPTER 18

Very early on a Saturday morning, Roger headed toward Fergus Falls to view the progress on his 1960, and Joey accompanied him. Contrary to his preferences, Roger had selected an interstate highway as the fastest way to get to their destination. He knew of several exits where diners and cafés were located that served excellent food. After a stop to fill the travelers with biscuits and gravy, they settled in for the trip.

As the friends traveled the boring interstate highway, Joey seemed preoccupied. "Penny for your thoughts," Roger said.

"Oh, it's all these open cases. Gordy Flowers was shot while running, and Dean Tyler was shot while working at his university office, and Rebecca Whelk committed suicide in her office. These three recent deaths seem very different, but I have a hunch that they are somehow connected."

Roger shrugged as if to say, *Certainly I have no idea.*

"You worked with Professor Whelk," Joey said. "Does it make sense to you that she would commit suicide?"

He thought silently a moment. "On the surface, I suppose it does. She was always rather negative, snide, and mean-spirited, and when she was notified that she would not be granted tenure, she got worse—much, much worse."

"However…?"

"She was always active and filled with energy—more so lately. I can see her in my mind as I speak—striding down the hallway to make a sarcastic comment to someone. She certainly wasn't quiet."

"Bottom line. Based on what you know of Professor Whelk, did she commit suicide?"

"I would be surprised. I suppose it's possible that when she was alone she got depressed and was suicidal—I don't understand that kind of psychology. But there is something else. It seems very odd that she would get up early in the morning, dress for work, come over to the office, take out a folder of papers for a meeting, and then shoot herself."

"Did you notice if the papers and folder on the floor were for the meeting that she was supposed to attend?"

"Yes. If she wanted to shoot herself, why didn't she simply stay home and do it?

"Perhaps the gun was in her office."

"That doesn't explain why she took the trouble to get out the folder for the meeting."

"No," Joey sighed, "it doesn't."

"You know there were other people in the building early that morning."

"Yes, you and Nell Underwood. Were there others?"

"You should talk with my neighbor, Mr. Bickett. He told me that he was working on his mower in his garage early in the morning, and he had the garage door open and he had an unobstructed view of our building. He told me that he saw someone in a green shirt enter the building after Rebecca arrived. You know that every working day, Darrell Yorick wears a green shirt that resembles a bank note."

"Did Yorick and Whelk know one another?"

"I dimly remember her saying something about how she refused to go to dinner with a wealthy banker."

As they drove into Fergus Falls and approached the Pretty Cars shop, Roger pointed to the diner across the street. "You'll love the hamburgers there."

In the shop, Roger introduced Joey to Mr. Prettyman. "I'm glad to meet Roger's co-pilot. Let's go look at his car."

The body had been painted and it was still sitting in the paint booth. Under the many bright lights, the turquoise color simply glowed. "Wow," Roger said. "It sure looks different from what I saw the last time."

"Yes. We repaired the imperfections in the fiberglass and replaced some of the panels. When we were happy with the full body, we coated it with gel coat to seal the fiberglass. We made that coat fairly smooth and removed any really large-scale surface unevenness, but we didn't want to make it so smooth that it would be more perfect than it could possibility have been in 1960."

Fred Farmer had walked over to join them. "As we discussed the last time you were here," he said, "I sprayed a polyurethane paint so that it looks like the original lacquer. I would say it looks quite 1960-ish." He walked around to the rear of the car. "There is a little bit of bumpy surface, orange peel, here on the rear panel. Remember, you agreed that there should not be a total absence of obvious orange peel since that might constitute an over restoration!"

Roger nodded and glanced at Joey. In an attempt to be agreeable, the sheriff also nodded and murmured, "Yes, I can see that." He had no idea what he was supposed to see.

"Your frame is over here," Fred said. They moved to the other side of the shop. "We scraped and sandblasted it, and then coated it with original type materials. We replaced all of the parts of the brake system. The brake lines are stainless steel. These stainless lines are stronger and last longer and therefore are safer. They were available in 1960, and if you get any deductions based on them, I would like to know it! This frame, the rolling stock, as I call it, is finished."

"Let's talk about your engine," Mr. Prettyman said. In an adjoining room, Roger found his engine disassembled. "We have cleaned everything, and we are ready to rebuild it. The only question we have is whether you want the old style valves and valve seats that require a flow of gasoline containing tetraethyl lead."

Roger nodded to acknowledge the question. "I could buy leaded gas at the local airport, but that's not always convenient. Let's go with newer valves and hardened valve seats so that I can use common unleaded fuel."

"Good. That's what I would recommend. Aside from your valves, which, of course, are impossible to see inside the heads, everything on your engine and drive train is correct and typical for this year and model: the manifolds, carburetors, distributor, water pump, transmission, and rear end."

"There are a few more minor points," Fred said. "In 1960, when your engine was painted, the intake and exhaust manifolds were in place. Therefore, there always was some orange paint overspray on the manifolds. Nowadays, any good engine builder would paint the block and heads before the manifolds were installed. Do you want overspray or not? "

"That's a tough one. On the one hand the orange paint (or the lack of it) on the aluminum intake and the bare cast iron exhaust is immediately obvious as soon as the hood is opened. And it also looks sloppy." Roger thought a few moments. "Let's do what we did with the orange peel. Have some overspray, but don't overdo it."

"Okay. Next, in 1960, the exhaust pipes extended exactly to the edge of the openings for them in the bumper—not beyond the edges of the bumper. Well, you will get some blackening of the bumper if they are aligned in that way. If you extend them about a half inch beyond the bumper, you can avoid the soot, but, remember, that was not the original position."

"That's an easy one. I can clean the bumper. Align the exhaust pipes exactly to the edge of the bumper as they would have been in 1960."

"Next, do you want gold or silver hood and deck-lid emblems? They were gold in 1960, but now even GM supplies only silver. They say that the emblems were originally silver and the sun changed the color to gold."

"Is that what happened?"

"Probably not. We could try to find gold in a salvage yard, but they are likely to be scuffed and dull."

"Try to find gold." Roger laughed, "Always go for the gold."

"Last question. Both of your red plastic taillight lenses are cloudy or foggy. We simply can't find new exact replacements. Do you want us to try to polish the old plastic? Or should we buy the closest replacements we can?"

"Try to repair the originals. Unless they're hopeless, I'd rather have them than differing replacements."

"I think we've covered everything. Remember, we're attempting to make the car as much like it was when it rolled off the assembly line, but we are not NCRS judges, and we are bound to miss a few things."

"But they should be minor things?"

"Yes, very minor."

"I can deal with that. So, are you on schedule?"

Mr. Prettyman looked at Fred, and he nodded. "Yes. Barring something significant that we can't foresee, you can pick up your car on September 1."

As Mr. Prettyman headed to the bathroom with his toothbrush, Fred walked the two men to the door. "Are you going to have lunch at the diner?"

"Yes. I told Joey about the great hamburgers."

"They have a new burger—I call it the double messy chiliburger, and I recommend it."

At the diner, Joey consumed two messy chiliburgers, and Roger had two triple onion-ring burgers. Both men ordered fries.

CHAPTER 19

The car show in Canton was large and famous. Its fame was not based so much on its size, but, rather, on the excellence of the judging. A really superior car was certain to win its class. As a result, the best cars were entered in the Canton show. The accurate judging was a great asset to anyone wanting to sell a show car. Potential buyers who knew that cars were Canton trophy winners would offer thousands of dollars more for them than they would have otherwise.

In the late morning the day before the Canton show, Roger whistled as he walked toward his garage to put his 2004 Corvette in show condition. It was not yet noon, and the temperature must have been in the 90s. He unlocked the side door on the garage and went directly to the air conditioner and turned it up to its highest setting. He knew it was wimpy to have cooling in a garage—so what if it's hot? Suck it up! However, he simply couldn't do his best work in an overheated environment, and the high heat was not good for his cars. When the garage had significantly cooled, he turned on halogen lights mounted on the ceiling directly over his Corvette. The bright lights shining on the yellow car made every speck of dust and every smear very obvious.

Except for newly-purchased vehicles, Roger never washed show cars with a hose, bucket, and soap. However, if he had not detailed a car for a while, he went over it from top to bottom. He first vacuumed the carpet and seats, and he put a brush on the end of the vacuum and went over the dash and places where dust could accumulate—such as the shift console.

He carefully went over the cloth top of the convertible with special preservative wipes—checking to be sure that all dust and tiny plant spores were removed and that there were no uneven-color spots—the top should be uniform tuxedo black.

He next turned his attention to the paint. He knew that the color and shine of the paint were the first things that a viewer noticed about a car. He dusted the car—just barely touching the fibers of the duster to the paint, and he made long swipes on the hood toward the front and swipes toward the back on the rear deck surface and up-and-down swipes on the sides of the car. In the same order, he went over the car with synthetic detail spray, being careful not to allow the spray to dry on the paint. Then, he sparingly applied polymer clear seal.

While the clear seal was drying, he applied tire dressing and went over the chrome wheels with a separate duster reserved for wheels. He polished them with detail spray and, finally, with a coat of clear seal. He cleaned the windows, both inside and outside, with GM foam glass cleaner and then polished them with Windex. Last, he finished the interior. He first sprayed leather cleaner, wiped it off, then rubbed conditioner on the seats and other leather portions of the interior. He also went over the dash and other molding with vinyl conditioner—being careful not to get the vinyl conditioner on the leather.

He stepped back and walked around the car. Several times he stepped forward to touch up a spot. The car looked good. Since the distance was short, he would drive the car to Canton, and he should need only to dust it and perhaps polish it a little with detailer to make it ready for judging.

On the day of the show, Roger had opened his garage and was about to leave to meet Em'ly and Nell at Em'ly's home, when her copper Corvette pulled into his driveway. "Hey, slowpoke, we couldn't wait for you any longer!" Em'ly yelled with a laugh. Roger waved and backed out to follow her car to Canton.

The show was so large that the cars overflowed the exhibition area in the city park and out onto the surrounding streets. Although their two Corvettes were in different classes, they were placed side by side on a shady side street. Nell had learned how to dust a show car, and she worked busily on the '55 while Em'ly used Windex to remove a few bugs from the front grill. Roger used detail spray to remove his bugs. Soon their Corvettes sparkled.

Roger noticed that his registration sheet that identified his entry number was not visible in his front window. "Em'ly, you don't happen to have some tape?"

"I sure do." She handed him a roll of clear tape.

"You're the seasoned automotive exhibitor who remembers everything!"

She simply smiled as the three sat in chairs in the shade behind the cars. They talked about the organization of the show and what a good job had been done by the weather committee—it was a beautiful sunny day. Roger reflected that they did not have to talk about car shows all day. He would ask Nell about her studies. "So, after two years of study, how do you like the university?"

"I like it! More than I thought I would. I especially enjoy my math courses, and I think I'll major in mathematics."

"You weren't so sure that you would like college when you started," Em'ly said.

"That's right. I thought I wasn't smart enough to go to college. The first semester I took only one course, and I was certain that I'd fail it. My teacher, Dr. Whelk, made me think that I would fail—one day as she was returning test papers she said to me in a sarcastic tone, 'I don't know why you're here.' I went home after class and cried. However, somehow I got a C in her literature course. I was very, very happy to pass.

"The next semester I enrolled in a business math course taught by Dean Tyler. I thought I might be able to get a decent grade from a male professor. Especially if I was nice to him."

"You mean if you flirted with him," Em'ly said.

"Well, yes. But it didn't work. He seemed repulsed by my smiles.—I don't know what was wrong with him—men have always thought that I was cute. Anyway, I found the course very easy;—the level of math was pretty simple, and I got an A on all of the tests and for the course. Then, the next semester, I took only math and physics courses, and I got As in both. This last semester I took a full load of five classes,—four math and science courses and another literature course,—not from Dr. Whelk!—and I got all As again. I was really proud of myself. I got a letter telling me that I was on some kind of honor roll!"

"I would say that you're indeed on a roll," Em'ly said.

"I feel as if I am. But as I look back, I wonder why Dr. Whelk gave me a C and why she was so mean to me."

"Do you know," Roger said, "that this would have been her last year teaching at this university?"

"I didn't know that, but it's probably good. Of course it's a terrible thing to say, but I have trouble feeling sad that she died." She looked at Roger. "Do you remember how critical she was about the way that I arranged your books?"

Roger nodded. "I remember."

"I'm glad that she's dead."

"Bitzer is headed our way," Em'ly said. "It looks like he's judging Corvettes." Bitzer was a regional director of car shows, and he was the manager of two car shows, and he was the dean of judges in the Midwest. Although he always seemed to be in a hurry, he was very thorough in his examination of cars. He was known to be a tough judge, but a fair one.

"Hi, Roger. I thought you now had a first-generation Corvette that you showed."

"I do have a 1960, but it's in the shop getting a full restoration so that it can compete with Em'ly's car." He smiled.

"Any Corvette would have a difficult time competing with her wonderful copper car," Bitzer remarked as he quickly moved to the front of Roger's car. He made lots of notes on one of two clipboards he carried. Although he moved in a rapid motion from position to position, he carefully scrutinized everything before him—the fit and finish on the front clip and hood, the chrome engine, the fenders and side of the car, the trunk lid and the trunk area, the rear including the exhaust. Then he examined each wheel as he moved to peer at the interior from both sides. He stood adding up his numbers.

Bitzer had been careful and diligent in judging Roger's modified car, but he was still more meticulous in examining Em'ly's stock Corvette. In particular, he consulted a manual to ascertain whether the numbers on the engine of her copper '55 were what they were supposed to be. It took him much longer to arrive at a total score for her car. As he moved toward the next Corvette, he was still bending over his clipboard.

Em'ly watched Bitzer moving into the distance. "I'll keep an eye on our cars if you two get us some food."

"Okay. What do you want us to get for you?"

"Surprise me."

Nell and Roger wandered through the rows of cars with hopeful owners sitting patiently behind them. Since Roger had campaigned a street rod many years earlier, he looked at the T-buckets and fenderless roadsters more carefully than some of the other cars. "These T-buckets are fad-Ts." Roger had slipped into his professorial teaching mode for a moment. "Except for the color of the paint, they all look alike."

Nell was clearly most interested in sports cars. She came to a complete stop and stood staring at a green Jaguar E-type convertible. "Someday," she said, "I want to own a Jaguar like that—or, even better, a yellow Corvette like yours." She grinned at Roger.

When they reached the edge of the city park where the majority of cars were displayed, their noses directed them toward a row of food stands. They found the food that they expected—hamburgers, hot dogs, corn dogs, and French fries—plus some unusual exotics such as onion rings, roasted turkey legs, and funnel cakes.

Nell wanted lots and lots of funnel cakes, and Roger ordered two hamburgers and a large order of onion rings. They got a turkey leg and a hamburger for Em'ly. Roger added three orders of French fries. In an attempt to neutralize the massive amount of calories and fats in the food, they purchased three diet drinks.

They walked back toward their cars very slowly so as not to spill any of the food. Nell looked up at Roger. "I shouldn't have said that I was glad that Professor Whelk was dead."

"I suppose not, but you had good reasons."

"That morning when I was waiting for you, I saw her walk down the hallway, and I didn't even want to look at her. I just turned away."

"Before I arrived that morning, did you see anyone else?"

"No. Er, wait. I thought I heard you coming up the stairs shortly after Professor Whelk, but when I glanced toward the stairs, it was some guy I didn't recognize."

"Do you remember what he looked like?"

"Not really. I just glanced at him as he came up the dark stairs, and as soon as I knew it wasn't you, I looked away.

"Where did he go?"

"I think he went in the same direction as Professor Whelk, but I didn't really watch him.

Roger considered. Nell might have seen the same man in a green shirt that Mr. Bickett noticed.

They walked past a series of modified Corvettes. Many of them were cars that Roger didn't recognize from other shows. They must be from Minnesota and surrounding states. A new dark red metallic Z06 was unusually impressive.

Em'ly was delighted with the fried turkey leg, but she looked with disdain at the hamburger, and she tossed it to Roger. The three of them ate, told funny stories, and ate some more. They were enjoying themselves.

As is usual at large shows, the announcement of awards was delayed and then delayed more. At last, the public address system that had been booming '50s music all day called the exhibitors together. Em'ly won first place in the stock Corvette division. The show director praised her car as "the best restored Corvette on the prairie."

Roger was a bit surprised that his Corvette took first place in the modified division—he thought the red car would win it. He wondered if he had gotten the award because he knew Bitzer, the judge. However, he thought as he looked at his chrome and yellow car shining in the sun, it did look pretty good.

As they were packing up their show bags, Roger told Em'ly, "It won't be much longer until I have my 1960 completely restored. When I get it back, let's both enter an official

NCRS show. There is one in Rochester, Minnesota, this fall."

Em'ly's 1955 had received official judgments of Top Flight previously at NCRS shows, but she had recently repaired and replaced several minor things on her car, and she was interested in a new NCRS assessment. "I would enjoy that," she said.

As he led the way back home, Roger thought about what Nell had told him. A man she did not recognize entered the Arts and Sciences Office Building shortly after Rebecca had gone to her office. Would he turn out to be her killer?

CHAPTER 20

"Have you ever seen Alfred Hitchcock's movie *Strangers on a Train*?" Roger asked Joey.

"Of course not. Do you think I hang out at classic film festivals in art theaters?"

The two men were lounging in Roger's comfortable garage late in the afternoon on a perfect August day. The garage door was open allowing a few colorful leaves to blow along the checkered floor. Roger thought the leaves looked like soldiers charging into battle. The late summer air was dissolving the scents of oil and car polish.

"I'll recount the plot of the movie. Two men who are complete strangers from very different walks in life happen to meet on a train. Both men have someone in their life they wish were dead. They agree to each commit the murder that the other wants. In that way, the man with an obvious motive could establish an iron-clad alibi, and even if suspicion were to fall on the actual killer, there would be absolutely no motive."

"Are you telling me this simply to entertain me?"

"Naturally, I always want you to be entertained, but I am recounting this plot for another reason. It occurred to me that this might be how Gordy Flowers and Dean Tyler died."

Joey sat up and thought about what Roger had just said. These were rather deep waters.

Roger continued to explain, "Ben Flowers stood to benefit significantly from the death of his wealthy brother, Gordy. Rebecca

Whelk greatly disliked her dean for denying her tenure. So, just like *Strangers on a Train*, Rebecca and Ben made an agreement. Rebecca killed Gordy, and Ben killed Dean Tyler. Remember that Gordy was shot with a .22, and we know that Rebecca bought a .22 in Connecticut. Dean Tyler was killed with a .38, and when Ben was in Texas, he purchased such a gun, and he often has it with him."

"Did Professor Whelk and Ben know one another?"

"Both of them acted in a community play, and they were noticed talking confidentially." Roger knew that there were some problems with the movie-plot theory, but he didn't want to mention them. Perhaps they could be resolved.

Joey looked as if he did not find Roger's idea very convincing, but it might be worthy of consideration. "We have the .22 that was found next to Rebecca's body. We can test it to determine if it was the gun that fired the shots that killed Gordy Flowers. We can ask for Ben's .38 and test to see if it was used on Dean Tyler. I suppose that we will need a warrant; in these days of TV law-and-order shows, no one hands over anything to the police without a warrant."

The Corvette clock on the garage wall gave out a loud exhaust roar to indicate that it was six o'clock. Joey knew that he should get home, but he wanted to think through this new theory.

"According to your idea, Professor Whelk made this agreement, bought a gun, actually shot Ben's brother, and then a few months later she shot herself with the same gun. Isn't that a little odd? I mean, she has succeeded in committing the perfect crime, so she promptly kills herself."

"Yes," Roger couldn't help laughing. "It does seem odd when you put it that way. However, who knows what was going through her mind? And, anyway, are you sure her death was suicide?"

"Hmmm. There are indications that it was not suicide; she was preparing to go to that meeting."

"She left home dressed for school, and when she got to her office, she hung up her coat and scarf, took out some papers and the folder for the meeting."

"And, according to this movie theory, Dean Tyler was killed because he had denied tenure for Professor Whelk…but, wait a minute. Didn't you tell me that Dean William Tyler was not her dean?"

"Yes. That is another problem with this theory. Tyler was dean of the Business School, and Rebecca was a member of the College of Arts and Sciences."

"And Professor Whelk had no reason to dislike Tyler?"

"As far as I know."

"So why would she make an agreement with Ben Flowers to kill Dean Tyler?"

"I don't know. Perhaps he didn't hear the name correctly. Maybe he got mixed up. For all I know, he might have been drunk. I don't know how such a mistake could be made."

"And does this idea have anything to do with Professor Whelk's death? Do you think that she felt so bad that Ben had screwed up that she killed herself?"

"You're making fun of me!"

"A little."

"Well, stop it. I'm serious."

"Or perhaps Ben was angry that he had shot the wrong dean, and he blamed Professor Whelk for his mistake, and he went to her office and struggled with her and shot her with her own gun?"

"You're still making fun of me, but you raise an interesting point. For whatever reason, someone might have gone to Rebecca's office that morning and argued with her and perhaps struggled with her and took her gun away from her and shot her with it."

"I must get home or I won't get any supper. I'll try to run the tests on the guns soon and let you know the results."

The two men continued talking as they slowly walked out of the garage toward Joey's car. "My 1960 should be finished in Fergus Falls next week, and I plan to pick it up on Saturday. Do you want to come along?"

"Sure. I enjoyed the hamburgers from the diner across the street."

Before dawn on Saturday, Roger attached his enclosed trailer to the hitch on his Hummer, and he crossed and connected the safety chains. When he stopped clanking and looked up, he found Joey was standing watching him.

"Let's get on our way." The men piled into the Hummer and slowly pulled away. Traffic was light, and they made only one stop to refuel and eat a light breakfast. Both of them left room for the burgers they knew they would enjoy in Fergus Falls.

Soon they were back on the road again. "Did you do any more thinking about the movie-plot theory of the killings?" Roger asked.

"We did test the .22 that was found next to Professor Whelk in her office, and it is the same gun that was used to shoot Gordy Flowers."

"Do you know whether that is the same .22 that Rebecca purchased in Connecticut?"

"I assumed it was her gun because we found it next to her in her office and since you said that she bought such a gun, but we don't know it's hers. Who sold it to her?"

"A man named Tom Weed. He owns Weed and Duryea Hardware in New Canaan, Connecticut."

"I'll find out if it's the same gun."

"But, in any case, do you think that there might be something to my crazy movie-plot idea?"

"Maybe. Did you say that someone saw Ben and Professor Whelk talking?"

"Yes, my office assistant, Nell Underwood—you talked with her. She said that she does makeup for community theater, and last year she worked on *Arsenic and Old Lace,* and Ben and Rebecca acted in that play, and she saw them talking. She said they were talking very quietly and privately, and she thought they were becoming close friends."

"Were they close friends?"

"It didn't appear so, and his sister, Em'ly, said she didn't realize that Ben even knew Rebecca."

"So, they were talking privately, but they wern't close friends. Hmmm. Your movie-plot theory sounds better and better."

"Did you test Ben's .38 to see if it was the gun that shot Dean Tyler?"

"No. I couldn't think of a pretext to ask for it, and I didn't want to accuse him of a crime."

As they arrived in Fergus Falls, Joey wondered, "Will your car look really different?"

"I suppose it will look much the same, but greatly improved—something like a person who has had a facelift." They pulled into the parking lot by the side of Pretty Cars, Inc. "I am so anxious to see my car that I'm a pack of nerves."

CHAPTER 21

Master mechanic Fred Farmer was just pedaling his bike up the driveway as Roger and Joey arrived. It was an old bike that squeaked and rattled and seemed about ready to fall apart. They waited as he leaned the bike up against the side of the building, and he didn't bother to lock it.

"You must be here to take the patient home."

"Yes."

"I think you'll find that she's perfectly recovered and exactly what you wanted."

When they went into the shop, Roger could not spot his turquoise car, but there was a car near the door that was protected with a soft felt car cover. Mr. Prettyman joined them in front of the covered car.

"Are you ready to see our handiwork?" he asked.

"I'm more than ready."

Mr. Prettyman stood on one side of the car, and Fred was on the other side, and they carefully lifted the cover and folded it over on itself to remove it without sliding it across the paint. "Behold the perfectly restored 1960 Corvette!"

Roger grinned as he walked around the car examining it. The Tasco Turquoise paint had a depth that made it seem to glow—yet it was not the shiny wet look of modern base coat/clear coat polyurethane paint. When Roger looked down the sides of the car, the paint was smooth and straight with just a hint of waviness that made the bodywork authentic. He squatted down to look at the paint under the rear bumper—as they had agreed, there was a little obvious roughness, a little orange peel. He grinned up at Fred. "It's not over restored!"

The chrome on the car was perfect from the front grill teeth to the rear bumper exhaust exits. It glistened in the illumination of the shop lights, and Roger thought about how much more light would be reflected from the natural sun. He opened the driver's door and sat in the driver's seat and smiled and frequently nodded as he looked over the dash, carpet, and seats. He unlatched the hood and got out and tipped the hood forward and looked at the engine. Again he smiled and nodded at the correct orange paint—with some overspray on the aluminum intake manifold. As he walked around the car again, he glanced at the taillights. "Are those my original plastic lenses?"

"Yes, we were able to clean and buff them so that they look like new."

"It's beyond belief."

He looked down at the exhaust pipes that were perfectly aligned with the bumper and then walked over to where Mr. Prettyman stood watching him. He shook his hand and said, "You guys perform magic. Thank you."

"It's a pleasure working with an owner like you who knows what he wants. Come into my office and I'll give you a detailed description of what we've done."

Joey was left standing next to Fred Farmer. Both of them were looking at Roger's car. Joey said, "It looks nice, but it doesn't look like a modern car."

"It's not supposed to. It looks like a Corvette that just rolled off the assembly line in 1960."

Joey nodded rather vaguely.

Roger soon emerged from Mr. Prettyman's office looking more like a kid who had just won a little league trophy than like a man who had just written a very large check. "Let's take the car for a spin," he said to Joey, "and then we can have a burger and head home."

When Roger and Joey sat in the car, they looked around at the spotless interior. "It actually smells like a new car," Joey said.

When Fred had opened the overhead door, Roger started the car. The engine purred so softly that he had to turn his head and listen carefully to hear it. When he carefully let out the clutch, the car moved silently toward the open door. "It also runs like a new car," he said to Joey.

The two men rolled down the side windows and waved to Mr. Prettyman and Fred Farmer as they pulled out into the parking lot. As Roger shifted into second gear and then into third, he said, "Shifting now feels like moving a wooden spoon in a tub of butter. Nice." As Roger drove, Joey noticed that he was driving very carefully and leaving a generous distance between the shining Corvette and nearby traffic. Heads turned and stared at the turquoise car as it passed.

They soon returned to the Pretty Cars parking lot and loaded the car into Roger's trailer. Roger very carefully inched the car into the dark trailer as Joey directed him with hand signals. Roger got out of the car and stood at the back of the trailer looking at his car. "I'm glad I bought this Corvette, and I'm glad I had it restored."

In the diner, Joey ordered two waffle burgers. He thought the waffles would be small—the size of regular burger buns—however, the burgers were huge—the size of regular waffles. Roger had two ham and cheese hamburgers—a combination of two favorite sandwiches. Joey took his time savoring his hamburgers and munching a side order of French fries. Roger seemed in a hurry to finish his food.

When they arrived back in Madison, Joey again directed Roger as he inched the new car out of the trailer. He carefully drove it into a space he had prepared in his garage. It was crowded in there, but Roger had made sure there was plenty of room for the 1960. He walked around his car, smiling broadly.

"Don't you want to take your new car for a drive?" Joey asked.

"No! I want to dust it, and clean it, and polish it. I want to see it looking absolutely, absolutely perfect—which it will."

Joey waved as he turned and walked to his car. He smiled to himself about the obsession of his friend.

After hours of cleaning and polishing a car that really didn't need much effort to look very good, Roger took a last look, set the alarm on the garage, shut off the lights, and took a long look at his 1960 as he closed the door. Inside his home, he finished re-reading a novel he would be teaching the next week, and he turned on the TV and half-heartedly watched an old movie and went to bed dreaming of his new car.

First thing on Monday, Roger went to his bank. Because of a large sum that was bequeathed to him by a great aunt, Roger was financially comfortable regardless of his buying another Corvette and spending a significant amount restoring it. However, he needed to transfer some money out of a long-term account to use for daily expenses.

On a previous visit to his bank, he had been waiting to talk with a minor bank officer when Darrell Yorick offered to help him. Perhaps he talked to Roger because he was a fellow Corvette owner and exhibitor. Roger didn't know, but he thought he would approach him rather than try to see the overworked officer. He knocked tentatively at the open door of Yorick's office.

"Ah, Roger. Come in, come in and sit down," he said in a friendly tone. Roger noticed that

Yorick was again wearing a green shirt with a weave that reminded him of a dollar bill.

The bank president smiled and nodded agreeably as Roger explained his finances. He explained that he had just paid for the complete restoration of a 1960 Corvette, and the check he had written completely depleted his checking account. As on the previous visit, Yorick discouraged cashing in a large CD, but rather advised him to borrow against the CD for the needed operating capital. Roger smiled at the term "operating capital." As if he were a struggling grocery store. Yorick called an assistant into his office and asked him to prepare the proper forms.

Yorick leaned back in his chair as a preface to chatting while the underling did the formal paperwork. He searched his mind for a moment for an appropriate topic that his customer might find of interest. "I can well understand your enthusiasm for Corvettes. As you know, I have a Corvette, but my real passion is my gun collection. I recently found another Smith and Wesson .38 Special that had been used for police service, and I had to buy it. I started by collecting small-caliber pistols, especially the .22, but now I have guns of all calibers."

Roger nodded and tried to look interested. "You see," Yorick continued, "most police departments have replaced their .38 Specials with .40 caliber weapons, and thus there are police-issue guns that are sometimes available for collectors. Listen, gun shows can be a gold mine for this type of thing."

Dr. Strong felt as if he were being patronized, and he was glad to see the bank official return with his papers. He was further patronized by being told to sign where there was a large X, as if he could never have figured that out by himself, and he was told that his checking account balance would be increased.

As the underling withdrew with the papers, Yorick stood up behind his desk—

thus indicating that Roger's audience with the bank president was over. Roger found Yorick an unpleasant person to deal with, and he reflected that there certainly were good reasons that Rebecca would not go out with him. That thought gave him an idea. He hesitated a moment and then spoke. "I'm sure you are saddened by Rebecca Whelk's death. She told me that you and she were acquainted."

It was a bombshell. Yorick's color changed as he looked straight at Roger as if to inquire exactly what he knew. He stammered a little and mumbled, "I knew her slightly." He put his arm behind Roger and guided him—almost pushed him—out of his office.

When Roger was outside he reflected that he had claimed more than he actually knew. He had overheard Rebecca say that she had refused to go to dinner with a wealthy banker, but she had not said it was Yorick, however, apparently Roger had correctly guessed the identity of the mystery banker.

CHAPTER 22

Roger had mixed feelings about what he should do with his 2004. It was a wonderful Corvette, and he enjoyed driving it and showing it, and he wanted to continue to show it, but, of course, he also wanted to show his newly-restored 1960, and it was not practical for one person to show multiple cars in the same show. Moreover, now that the 1960 was permanently in his garage, he could use a little more room. Perhaps he could sell the 2004 to someone who would appreciate the car and give it the same kind of care that he had given it. He hoped it would also be owned by someone who would exhibit it. He wondered if he should advertise it for sale.

Roger had not shown his restored 1960 to Em'ly, and he was eager to do so. He drove to her home, parked next to her house in the long sweeping driveway, and honked insistently. When she came out of the house, he simply sat in his car grinning.

"Oh, Dr. Strong, your car is wonderful!"

He got out of the car and stood next to her as the two looked at the Corvette in silence for a few moments. "Let me take a closer look at it," she said. She walked around the car, stared down its length, peered at the interior, and looked under the car. "I'm not an NCRS judge," she said, "but this looks like a Top Flight Corvette to me!"

"I hope so."

"Do you still want to enter it in the NCRS show in Rochester?"

"Yes, definitely."

"Are you going to continue to show your 2004?"

"Well, I wish I could, but the more I think about it, am not sure that I can. I want to focus on showing the 1960 now that I have gone to the trouble and expense of restoring it, and I can't also do justice to showing the 2004."

"Do you intend to sell the 2004?"

"If I did sell it, I'd like to see the new owner show it. A thought crossed my mind, and I would like your opinion. Nell has mentioned several times that her dream is to have a car like my 2004, and you have taught her the ropes of showing cars. Is there any way it could be arranged for her to buy the car?"

Em'ly opened the passenger door of the 1960 and sat down to think. "That's an interesting question." She spoke in an even, low tone. "Of course it's a wonderful idea. Nell's preparing the car for shows and exhibiting it would keep her occupied and out of trouble. It's a great project—I suppose."

"You don't sound very enthusiastic about the notion."

"I am thinking about the financing. Nell shouldn't be given the car, because that would be counter-productive to making her responsible. However, she has a little money—she has a scholarship, and she doesn't absolutely need the job in your office. I pushed her to take that position to teach her good work habits and responsibility. If someone would finance the purchase, she probably could make the payments."

"Should I finance it? Or, what about you?"

"No, you are her boss, and I am her friend and big sister. A loan from us would be too much like a gift—again, counter-productive to responsibility."

"What if we sent her to Yorick's bank?"

"His loan officers would probably turn down her financing."

"Perhaps one or both of us could talk with Yorick and tell him that we want to continue to do business with his bank, but we also want our friend Nell to get a loan from his bank."

"Nell would be embarrassed and probably wouldn't accept the loan if she knew what we'd done."

"We would have to ask Yorick to keep our little extortion a secret from Nell."

"You've come up with the perfect plan."

"Thanks."

"Dr. Strong, for a professor of arts and sciences, you think a lot like a financial manipulator."

"I'm not sure that's a compliment, but thank you, if it is."

They both laughed.

In the next days, both Em'ly and Roger talked with Yorick. Roger found that, after the banker had given the matter of Nell's financing a moment's thought, he agreed surprisingly readily. Roger assumed that a bank president was always eager to keep good customers happy.

When matters were prepared at the bank, Roger had a delightful conversation with Nell. He explained that he now wanted to devote all of his attention to showing his restored 1960 Corvette, and thus he wanted to sell his 2004. He insisted that it would be put in the hands only of someone who would properly care for it and continue to enter it in car shows. And he thought that the ideal new owner would be Nell Underwood.

She looked at him with wonder and disbelief, and she laughed with pleasure, but she shook her head. "I can't afford to buy that car from you."

Roger explained that she probably could afford it. He described the car as a worn-out show car and set the price accordingly. They both knew that there was nothing worn-out about the Corvette, but she didn't challenge his statement. She should talk with a loan officer at Yorick's bank, and they would work out the details.

When Nell repeated the conversation to Em'ly, the two of them laughed with pure glee and praised Dr. Strong. Em'ly said that she had unused space in her garage next to her 1955, and Nell was welcome to work on the 2004 there and, of course, store it there.

Nell talked with President Yorick, and the following day, Roger met Nell at the bank, and they spent about an hour watching a loan officer shuffle papers and tell them to sign where there was an X. He shook Nell's hand and announced, "Here's your payment schedule. You are now the owner of a Corvette." He shook Roger's hand and said, "Your account has been credited."

Nell rode with Roger to his garage to transfer the Corvette to Em'ly's garage. She was clearly very excited to own the car, and she was eager to drive it, and she could hardly wait to enter it in a show. However, as she mentioned the bank arrangements, a shadow came over her face, and she was silent a few moments.

"Dr. Strong, the bank president said something very strange to me. He and I talked about the terms of the loan for the car, and he said he would approve it—he had not even checked my credit rating. He said he would set the interest rate very low and the monthly payments were also low. Then he said that he was sure that I would appreciate the loan, and we would be on the friendliest possible terms, and therefore, I wouldn't bother to mention that I had seen him in your building the morning that Professor Whelk died. He stared at me, and without thinking, I said, 'Of course not.' At first I didn't know what he was talking about, but later I wondered if he was the man I saw in the hallway that morning. He must have been that man!" She gave a shudder.

"Apparently he was. He obviously thought that you could identify him."

"I really didn't look at him."

"He doesn't know that."

"What should I do?"

"You will have to tell the truth. If Yorick has done nothing wrong, the truth won't hurt him."

Nell   slightly   nodded   in uncertain agreement.

In preparation for entering his 1960 for the first time in an event sponsored by the National Corvette Restorers Society, he cleaned and inspected the car. He hummed to himself. He always enjoyed puttering with his cars—with this one in particular. As he worked, repeatedly he thought, "This car performs and looks exactly as it did when it rolled off the St. Louis assembly line in October, 1959."

Joey came in the side door and stood watching Roger dust the hood of the 1960. "Couldn't you put on that clear seal stuff and make the paint shine more?"

"I probably could do that, but then the car would not have the deep fuzzy glow of the original paint. I have to keep telling myself that the NCRS is looking for what appears typical—in the sense of correct and original. Because I'm an unrepentant hot rodder, it does run against the grain that an NCRS Corvette shouldn't be over-restored—this car should not look better or operate better than it could have in 1960."

Joey nodded as if he did not quite understand that philosophy, but he did not have sufficient interest to discuss it further. He opened two bottles of beer from a six-pack that he had brought with him, and he put the others in the refrigerator. He handed a bottle to Roger and took a swig from the other bottle and put it down on the coffee table made from a stack of tires. He sank into the well-worn sofa.

"I'm glad you swung by today," Roger said as he sat on a stool at his workbench.

"I know, I know. You want to tell me about the matching numbers on your fan belt and hoses."

"Yes! I am so excited to have hose numbers 144787 and 144788!"

Joey looked at his friend with mock disappointment. "And I thought that you wanted to tell me something that would help solve our two and one-half open murder cases."

"Why 'one-half'?"

"Gordy Flowers, Dr. Tyler, and, perhaps Dr. Whelk. Her death has not yet been officially classified as murder—thus two and one-half."

"Actually, I did learn some things that might be related to the one-half. I was talking to Darrell Yorick about transferring some funds in his bank, and I recalled that I once overheard Rebecca Whelk laugh that she had refused to go to dinner with a wealthy banker. I didn't know who the banker was, but I mentioned something to Yorick about his knowing Rebecca, and he got very flustered and hustled me out of his office."

Joey looked very interested.

"And remember that I told you that my neighbor, Mr. Bickett, saw someone in a green shirt enter our college building shortly after Rebecca went in. Did you talk to him?"

"Yes. He said exactly what you just said, but he was vague about the details. However, he was very specific about the benefits of mowing his lawn in the rain."

"I'm sure he was. The soil will be stimulated by the mowing, you know." Both men grinned. "Well, there is further confirmation that Yorick was in the building that morning. My office assistant, Nell, was waiting for me in the hallway, and she saw a man come up the stairs shortly after Rebecca had gone to her office. She simply glanced at him, and didn't think anything about it. However, when she talked to Yorick about getting a loan to buy my 2004, he readily granted the loan, and told her that they were pals and therefore she needn't mention seeing him in the building that morning."

"So he was there and he assumed that Nell could identify him."

"That's exactly what I thought."

The sheriff was silent, and he stood up and paced a short distance and returned. "Don't mind me. I'm adding up the evidence."

"And, Joey, did you know that Yorick has a gun collection?"

"Really? I can easily check to see what guns are registered to him."

"He told me that he had just purchased a .38 Police Special and he has several .22 caliber pistols."

"He told you that?"

"Yes, he was attempting to explain how we men have our excessive hobbies." Now Roger was silent for a moment. "Let me tell you what I can add up. Yorick disliked Gordy because his Corvette was putting Yorick's car in the shadow in shows and because of business deals. Yorick owns the same type of gun that killed Gordy. Yorick would have been humiliated that Rebecca would not go out with him, and he owns the kind of gun that killed her. And remember that Yorick had an argument with Bill Tyler, and he was shot with a .38—which Yorick owns.

"Taken together, Yorick had a motive to kill all three people, and he owns the matching weapon for each. We know he had opportunity in the case of Whelk. Someone wearing a green shirt was seen near the airport where Gordy was shot, and Yorick often wears a green shirt. We don't know that he had opportunity to kill Tyler, but since the dean was alone in his office, it wouldn't have been difficult."

Joey nodded and finished his beer. "I believe I need to talk to Mr. Yorick."

CHAPTER 23

Since Em'ly's 1955 had been judged in several NCRS events and had received Top Flight status, Roger asked her to tell him what to expect at the NCRS show in Rochester that he was about to enter. She told him on the phone that she and Nell were working on their cars in her garage and he was welcome to stop by. When he arrived, both overhead garage doors were wide open. From the clanging of tools and the clutter of parts and the flurry of activity, he thought he was entering a major hot rod garage. Em'ly's Corvette was on jack stands, and she had removed both wheels on one side, and she seemed to be cleaning the brake drums. Both doors of Nell's yellow Corvette were standing open, and she had removed one of the seats, and it was stripped to the bare frame and springs.

Roger stood in front of the car that he had formerly owned and watched Nell who carefully worked on the back of one of the seats. She seemed to understand the art of upholstery very well. She got up and stood next to Roger. "I must run down to the leather shop—I'll be right back." She gave him a flirtatious hip bump and smiled at him over her shoulder as she walked away.

Em'ly said, "That girl can certainly be a charming flirt."

"She's smart and—even more important— she has a powerful imagination. And, yes, she is a very cute flirt."

"Men find her irresistible."

"When we were sitting around at the Canton show, didn't Nell say that she tried to flirt with her business professor, Dean Tyler, and he wasn't impressed—he found her resistible."

"That's true. She and I had a long talk about him—she disliked him, but she kept her feelings hidden from him, of course, since she was doing well in his class, and she wanted a good grade. She was absolutely offended that Dr. Tyler seemed to scorn her. The only other man she seemed unable to attract was my brother Gordy. She tried to talk to him when she was doing makeup for 'Arsenic and Old Lace.' Gordy simply ignored her, she said. I think she disliked him, too, but she would not tell me that."

"So, aside from Dr. Tyler and Gordy, all of the other males find her charming. That's a pretty good percentage."

Em'ly nodded.

"But tell me what to expect at the NCRS show."

"I can give you a general overview. To start with, don't call them 'shows.' They are 'meets.' We're going to attend the NCRS North Central Chapter Meet. They are also generically called 'events,' but I have never heard them called 'shows.'"

"Okay."

"You will want to clean your Corvette—a clean car will be expected, and you don't want a bit of dirt mistaken for a flaw in a part. However, the evaluation will not be based on the car's cleanliness, as such. As you know, the judges will look at the whole car to see that everything appears and functions the way it did when it left the factory. It sounds clumsy to put it this way, but they want nothing to be 'not typical,' in the sense of not original or not correct.

"Each car will be examined by a lot of judges—at least ten. There are five teams with two judges on each. One team will score operations, another the interior, still another the exterior, the mechanical, and last, the chassis. You can't predict what order they will examine your car. There might also be some additional training judges or observer judges.

"Each car starts with a total of 4500 points. For each item or quality that is found not typical, a few points will be subtracted. A car must score at least 4230 points, that's 94 percent, to attain Top Flight status. In other words, in order to be Top Flight, your car can't have more than 270 points in deductions."

"Being able to have 270 points of deductions sounds like a lot, but I suppose it's not."

"It definitely isn't. Remember that the judges are inspecting every bolt and washer and every stitch of upholstery and every inch of the entire car—even the inside of the trunk and underside. You can win a lower flight designation by earning as little as 74 percent of the points—1125 points of deductions."

"I am looking for Top Flight."

"Of course. We all aim for the top."

"What score did your '55 receive?"

"The first time Gordy entered it in an NCRS meet, there were *oohs* and *aahs* from the judges because the car was so rare, and they were simply delighted to evaluate it. However, they found all kinds of deductions for hundreds and hundreds of points, and the car barely made Second Flight. Gordy and I replaced a few parts that were not original, and we repaired a lot of things.

"At the next event he entered, a regional meet, the '55 scored 91 percent—still Second Flight. He fixed some additional things and entered another regional meet, and won Top Flight—95 percent. He was delighted. Since I have shown the car, I have received another 95 percent and a 96 percent. These judges always find some deductions, and, actually, that's the great value of the events—you discover additional things that you can do to make your Corvette still more like the way it left the factory."

"How long does the judging take?"

"All day. Theoretically, your car could be judged in a few hours in the morning, but that simply never happens. A team descends on you, and the judges peer and mumble and make notes for a half hour or an hour or more, and then they talk briefly to the owner and move on and you wait and wait for another team—and so on. In any case, the rules require you to stay the whole day. You can't even wander away from your car—if the judges show up and the owner isn't there, they won't judge the car."

Nell came up behind them as they were talking. "I found the greatest leather. Look, they call it silver, but it is more like chrome, and it matches the chrome under the hood. I love it. Let me show you what I'm going to do."

She walked over to the seat she had removed from the car, and she draped the chrome leather around the outside of the seat frame, and she took some yellow leather from a box. "I took the car to the leather shop and I had them dye the leather to match the paint. They did a pretty good job."

She looked back and forth at Roger and Em'ly for agreement. They both nodded encouragingly and murmured, "Yes… very good."

"I'll upholster the main body of the bottoms and backs of the seats with the yellow leather, and I'll trim them with the chrome. They'll look like framed paintings. Now, I don't want the seats to stand out so much that they look like someone put the seats of another car in this one, so I'll do the interior accessories with the same pattern and colors—the grab bar, center console, shift boot, emergency brake boot, and door handle accents."

"Nell, that will be striking," Roger said. "Your father was certainly correct in saying that you have an eye for color. How did you learn to do upholstery?"

"I took a night course in a technical school—that was back when I didn't think I was college material. I cut class so often that I failed the course, and I had to take it a second time." She laughed. "However, I learned a great deal in taking it twice."

Both Roger and Em'ly looked back at the displayed leather on the seat and nodded in confirmation of Nell's good taste and upholstery skills.

Roger wanted another pair of eyes to look over his 1960 prior to his loading it in his trailer and taking it to the Rochester NCRS event. He asked Joey to stop and look at it.

Sheriff Bucket appeared as requested. "What duties do you have for me?"

"Look over my car very carefully and point out to me any spot or surface that looks like it needs cleaning." Roger handed his friend a light. "Start at the front, and I'll follow behind you with cleaning materials."

"Yes, sir." Joey peered at the toothy center grill and then at the side grills. " Here's something. Is this what you want me to point out?"

Roger looked closer and saw smears on a chrome headlight bezel. "Yes, exactly. The judges will be looking for flaws in the parts, and I don't want them to mistake a bit of careless polishing for a defective part."

"And there's a bit of dirt here in this wheel well—this is unacceptable."

"Okay. Thanks."

Joey shifted to the engine. "And here— look at this washer, and there is another! They are both dirty, and that dirt could be mistaken for a crack. And look at that bolt! This is a scandal! Oh, the shame and humiliation you must feel!" Joey was grinning—he was enjoying this far too much.

"Okay. I can do without the editorializing."

After more than an hour, Joey pointed out marks on the screws of the left taillight. "These marks will probably put your car in last place," he said quietly, and he announced, "I am finished."

"Thank you, Joey. Your keen eye has really been helpful. And " his tone changed to that of an announcer, "as a token of the appreciation from all of us, we would like to award to you this ice cold bottle of the finest beer in the garage!"

"I humbly accept this award on behalf of all who have worked so hard," Joey said as he grabbed the bottle, opened it, and took a big swig. He sank into his accustomed spot on the worn leather couch. Roger took a stool at the workbench.

"I noticed something the last few days," Roger said.

"What? A fly speck on your windshield?"

"No, I'm serious."

"So am I."

"Settle down or I'll take back your recently-won award."

"Ah, that threat gets my attention. Okay, I'm serious now."

"I hesitate to mention this, and it might really be a stretch, but it could be important. Someone might argue that Nell Underwood had a motive to kill Gordy Flowers, Bill Tyler, and Rebecca Whelk."

"Really?"

"Perhaps this is all silly and inconsequential."

"Tell me anyway."

"The first day that Nell worked in my office, she put my books in order of the colors of the spectrum. A few days later, Rebecca Whelk saw the books, and she ridiculed the arrangement—right in front of Nell. The poor girl was simply crushed."

"Do you think that's sufficient motive to kill someone?"

"I don't think so, but Nell was in the building that morning. And she does have a checkered past."

The sheriff mumbled something to himself. "What about the other two?"

"You might have observed that Nell is a bit of a flirt. Em'ly told me that Nell attempted to flirt with Tyler when he was one of her professors. Also, she flirted with Gordy Flowers when the two worked on a community play, and in both cases, Nell was rebuffed or ignored. No woman likes to be scorned."

"I'd have had no idea about this kind of thing. How did Em'ly know about these unsuccessful flirting attempts?"

"Nell told her, and Em'ly mentioned it to me. Em'ly has cultivated a close relationship with Nell as her Big Sister, and I gather that the two of them have long sisterly talks."

"I must look into this. Maybe Nell will flirt with me."

"I'm sure she will."

CHAPTER 24

As Roger connected the safety chains on his trailer to the hitch on his Hummer, he was nervous. He had entered cars in many shows, but having his newly-restored 1960 Corvette judged in an NCRS meet was different. He and Joey drove over to Em'ly's home and found Ben at the wheel of her truck that would pull the trailer containing her 1955. Nell and Em'ly jumped into the truck cab with Ben, and both vehicles headed for Rochester, Minnesota.

Roger thought that the variety of food that could be purchased on a road trip was one of the pleasures of travel, and he wanted to take advantage of as many roadside eateries as possible. It was not long before his stomach told him that it was time to eat biscuits and gravy, and he pulled into the parking lot of a small diner.

The five travelers stretched as they got out of the trucks and seemed happy to take a break. The biscuits they were served were small, but there were lots of them smothered in sausage gravy with many links of sausage on the side. About half way to Rochester, the group stopped for lunch at an Italian restaurant, and they enjoyed the spaghetti with enormous meatballs.

They entered Rochester late in the afternoon. At the motel, Nell and Em'ly shared a room, but each of the three men had a room to himself. As they were walking down the hall to their rooms, Ben stopped the sheriff. "As a professional, give me some advice. I have a revolver locked in the glove compartment of Em'ly's truck. Should I leave it there overnight, or should I bring it to my room?"

"What kind of gun is it?"

"Does it make a difference? It's a Smith and Wesson .38 Police Special."

Joey thought for a moment. "If it's locked up, it would probably be safe in either location, but it might be wise to bring it to your room overnight. You had better return it to the truck in the morning when you leave for the show, however, since during the day, a maid will be cleaning your room. When the gun is out there, keep the truck locked and lock the glove compartment as well." Ben nodded and turned back to get the gun from the truck.

The five travelers met minutes later for an early dinner at a colorful, brightly-lit pizza place. As they waited for their orders, Roger turned to Em'ly. "The schedule states that the NCRS judging starts at 8:00 a.m. How early do we need to arrive?"

"At least an hour before the start—perhaps more. We need to unload the cars, get registered, get the cars set up and dusted. We're only a few miles from the show site, but I think we should plan to leave the motel at 6:30." Accordingly, they ate and turned in early.

Roger left a wake-up call for 5:00 a.m. so that he would have plenty of time to shower, dress, and look over the NCRS materials that had been sent to him. When an event was important, he didn't like to rush to attend it.

The weather on the early fall day of the show could not have been more perfect. A day with light wind and temperatures in the 70s was predicted. Em'ly and Roger parked their trucks in a grassy lot as directed by volunteers. They drove their Corvettes into an adjoining blacktop parking lot. All of the first-generation cars were backed up in a staggered row near a fence. Looking around the lot, Roger saw that there were several dozen

Corvettes of each generation. He wondered if the large numbers would affect the judging, although Em'ly had told him that all the cars would be judged against standards and not compared one with another.

Because their cars had been trailered to the event, Em'ly and Roger needed only to dust their cars to make them ready for judging. Although most of the exhibitors set up chairs behind their cars, almost all of the owners were walking around and chatting with other owners. Exhibitors seemed to be much more interested in other cars than at any show that Roger had entered.

Roger walked along the row of early Corvettes, and he stopped in front of a red 1957. The car looked familiar. He turned and saw Pie Pryo walking back to his car. "Hey," Pie said, "It's good to see you. Did you bring the Turk to this event?"

"Yes, it's here. It has undergone some restoration since you saw it at the Village show. This is the first time it's been entered in an NCRS meet."

"Rosie here joins me in wishing good luck to the Turk. Did your friend enter her copper penny?"

"Yes, as a matter of fact. It's over there next to the Turk."

"Let's go look at both cars."

Pie remembered Joey, and he greeted him as "The Sheriff." Roger introduced Pie to his three colleagues, and he talked to them in the friendliest terms, but his real interest was Em'ly's Corvette. "I hope you don't mind if I call this magnificent car Penny. I can't help giving nicknames to cars, and this one is based on its color, obviously." Pie looked over the Turk, and he seemed to notice things that made him wince slightly, but he was silent about them. "This is a nice restored 1960," he said. He did not say that the Penny was a far, far nicer car, but he seemed to think that. He turned to look at it again. He seemed to discover wonderful proper parts and features everywhere he looked. He nodded his final judgment to Em'ly. "Your car is even better than I was told. It's simply magnificent. You should be very proud."

"I am. Of course, our brother did most of the initial restoration, and I am simply touching up a few minor items and exhibiting the car."

"Ah, I'd like to talk to that brother. Is he here?"

"No. He is dead."

"Oh. I'm sorry. An accident?"

"No, actually it was murder."

Pie didn't know what to say, so he simply repeated, "I'm sorry." He awkwardly turned and walked back to his car.

During the exchange, Ben seemed very uneasy and looked at the ground in a furtive manner. He walked to the back of the Penny. When Pie had left, the group stood silent for a few moments.

Nell was the first to speak. "Am I the only one who's hungry? Em'ly gets us out here before dawn with nothing to eat! I want food!" She looked at Em'ly with mock anger.

"Roger and I should stay here, owners are supposed to keep close to their cars, so Nell, Ben, and Joey, you must buy coffee and rolls for all of us. Get lots of rolls."

As the three left to scavenge for food, Em'ly told Roger, "Before we get our fingers all gooey from the rolls, we should remove the air cleaners and ignition shielding so that the engines are ready for inspection. We should probably also look over our cars one final time."

It was a good thing that Em'ly and Roger did remain with their Corvettes and got them ready for judging, because the team that covered the mechanical aspects of the cars arrived almost as soon as the others left in search of food. Roger immediately recognized one of the judges—Brayden, a

judge who had worked at Jerry's show and at
the Village show. Brayden's fellow judges were
large men who looked like NFL linebackers
in particularly good shape.

Brayden was chatting with his fellow
judges as they approached Roger's car. "I
would be honored to judge at the Nationals
this fall, but I simply can't be out of pocket
so much. I missed two weeks in June and
now I'll miss another week. Perhaps Bill can
judge—although he's not the brightest bulb
in the litter."

As before, Brayden immediately recognized
Roger's car. "Of course," he said. "This 1960
was a wonderful survivor when I last saw it,
and now it seems to be fully restored. It's a
pleasure to see it again in bright, new clothing.
As they say, you can treasure it twice, and not
cut your fun once."

Brayden and a fellow judge put fender
covers on both sides of Roger's engine, and
they carefully examined everything within

the engine bay. They used mirrors and small lights to peer at numbers stamped on the rear of the block, at the front of the block near the heads, and on other parts, and they compared them with numbers listed in manuals that they carried. Aside from a glance that Brayden gave to the tachometer on the dash, he confined his attention to the parts under the hood. His co-judge asked to examine the air cleaner and chrome shielding from the ignition that Roger had removed.

Brayden examined the carburetors closely and noted the numbers on the tags. He looked very closely at the coil and distributor. He seemed fascinated with the water pump and the hoses that were connected to it. Roger was surprised that these judges wanted to examine even very small parts such as the wing nuts from the top of the air cleaner. They peered at the throttle linkage and the wires that ran from the engine through the firewall.

The judges mumbled together and compared the notes that they had made on the sheets on their clipboards. Then Brayden talked with Roger to explain their judgments about the mechanical aspects of his car. "On the whole, this is a typical engine and drivetrain for a 270 horsepower 1960 Corvette. With this restoration, you hit it on the nail. However, there are a few deductions. First of all, the radiator cap is modern." Roger quickly turned his head to look at the cap—it was obviously new—he had not even thought about it previously. "The clamps on the heater hose that connects at the front of the intake manifold are not typical nor are the clamps on the bottom hose to the radiator. Throughout the engine, there are bolts that should be cadmium plated but are black or plain, and most of the lock washers are modern, smooth washers and not typical ones with a textured edge.

"This sheet details what I have just said. I will ask you to initial it at the bottom – you're not agreeing with our ratings you're simply acknowledging that we have discussed them with you." Roger did as he was asked. He was depressed that his engine had so many deductions.

"You will be mailed a copy of the judging sheets when all the scoring is done," Brayden said as he was about to walk off.

"And don't look so sad about this judging," Brayden added. "The great value to you of our judging is that you will now be able to easily make the recommended changes. Really, it's not rocket surgery."

Joey was standing close enough to overhear Brayden's comments, and he whispered in a light tone to Roger, "I tried to tell you about those odious washers!" Roger looked so dispirited that Joey wished he had kept his mouth shut.

Brayden and his fellow judges moved a few steps over to Em'ly's 1955. "Well," Brayden said. "This car sure throws a monkey at the wrenches in this class!" Roger thought it was impolite to observe the judges too closely as they worked over Em'ly's car, let alone to listen to their comments about her car, but he couldn't help noticing that they seemed to give her Corvette even more scrutiny than they had given his. They frequently consulted the books that they carried as if they had found something that was a rogue part, but almost immediately they would nod as if to say, "Oh, it is typical after all." Throughout the judging, Em'ly looked relaxed and confident. Finally, they talked with her, and she was nonchalant as she initialed the judging sheet.

As Brayden was about to walk away, he motioned to his fellow judges and said to Em'ly, "You are the kind of owner it is a pleasure to work with. Some Corvette folks are always angry over every deduction. It certainly is good to have these experienced judges with me; they block and tackle the irate owners."

Roger assumed from her attitude that Em'ly had very few deductions for her car, and he didn't care to ask her about her score. Instead, he said, "I suppose there will be a long wait until we see the next team of judges."

"Well, no," Em'ly said, "I think the judges for the exterior are working their way down our row as we speak." Roger looked up and saw judges examining a Corvette three cars away. When they arrived at his car, they spent most of their time looking down the length of his car to determine if the body was straight and to evaluate the qualities of the paint.

There was a long break for lunch. Ben, Joey, and Nell fetched enough corndogs to feed a moderate-sized army that was unusually hungry, and the five of them happily sat munching them in the shade of the metal fence.

About mid afternoon, just as Roger was thinking that this event was much longer and more tedious than most hot rod shows, another team appeared. They judged the operations of the car. They were interested in how the car started and idled. They asked Roger to use the turn signals, turn on the headlights, and to operate everything that was controlled from knobs on the dash. They had not moved on when the interior crew arrived. They examined the upholstery on the seats and door panels while the operations judges were talking to Roger. Moments later the chassis crew moved in. They were very curious about the underside of Roger's car. Both judges put cardboard down and slid under the car to examine the frame and other parts—especially the transmission and differential. Roger could hear them talking to each other under the car, and occasionally there were sounds of scraping or tapping.

It was well after 5:00 when they concluded their work.

As the five met for dinner, everyone was exhausted from the long day. In addition to being tired, Roger was so depressed about his scores that he looked as if he could punch someone at any moment. They were hungry, and everyone ordered a steak and sat waiting.

"So," Joey said. "Tell us why you look so glum."

"I have entered dozens and dozens of car shows. I have shown two completely different hot rods—one of which I campaigned for end-of-year awards, plus I showed a modified Corvette. I have a garage full of trophies. Of course I've had disappointments, but nothing like this. Nothing!

"The judges gave me a boatload of deductions, including full deductions in five areas. The radio doesn't work, the cigarette lighter doesn't get very hot, the wipers move funny, a taillight is dim, the master brake cylinder is the wrong color, and I have the wrong size steering wheel. All that plus I have modern lock washers! I'm sure I received so many deductions that I didn't even have enough points to make Third Flight. I couldn't even make it into the also-ran bracket!"

Roger had to stop talking—his anger was a black cloud within him that would swell and grow until he made it stop by thinking calming thoughts. He looked down at the table and then into the distance and took a deep breath.

Em'ly looked dissatisfied with herself. "Dr. Strong, I should've warned you better. When you enter your Corvette in its first NCRS event, of course the judges are going to find all kinds of deductions. I'm sorry, but that's a good thing—because when you get the judging sheets, you'll know exactly what to change and repair. You'll have a descriptive list. In fact, it's a prescriptive list."

Roger looked at her as if he recognized the truth of Em'ly's observations, and they were almost exactly what Brayden had told him, but he was not going to be consoled. He was still angry. He knew he was being childish, but he couldn't help it. However, a glass of wine and a well-grilled filet mignon did a lot to lift his spirits, and he was soon joking with the rest of his party.

The two trucks pulling first-generation Corvettes in trailers started for home early the next morning. When they arrived back in Madison, Roger stopped in front of Em'ly's house. He wanted to explain something to her. "Em'ly, you did tell me what to expect from NCRS judging, and I simply didn't listen. You told me that every little thing would be judged, and I didn't believe you. I am determined to fully restore that turquoise stinker of mine within an inch of its life, and it *will* win Top Flight!"

"That's the right attitude, and with that attitude you will succeed."

While Roger and Em'ly were talking, Joey walked over to Ben. "You said that you have a .38 Police Special revolver. Our department used them at one time, but now we've completely switched to .40 caliber automatics. Last week, I wanted to make a simple comparison between the two guns, and I couldn't find a .38 anywhere. Could I borrow yours for a day or two?"

Ben hesitated and looked reluctant, but he didn't know how to turn down the sheriff. "Well, I suppose." He unlocked the glove compartment and handed the revolver to Joey.

"Thanks."

When Roger got back in the Hummer, Joey said, "I think I just got an important piece of the puzzle of three deaths."

CHAPTER 25

The night Roger arrived home from the Rochester event, he thought about what he needed to do to earn NCRS Top Flight status. He now knew much more about what the judges were looking for and how their minds worked. He started looking in catalogs for parts that would restore his 1960 in ways that would avoid the deductions in the future. The next morning he called Corvette parts companies and Corvette salvage yards and ordered a variety of items from a reconditioned radio to period-correct hose clamps. In the following weeks, he received a series of shipments, and some of them contained parts that were exactly what he needed, but others had to be returned because they were not what they were represented to be.

He re-read all the literature that he had about restoring first-generation Corvettes— both from NCRS and from other sources. He ordered two additional books that he did not own. He learned that the bolts, nuts, and washers on his Corvette had three kinds of finish—silver cadmium, black phosphate, or gold cadmium. In a neighboring city, he discovered a blacksmith shop that could plate bolts, nuts, and most any part so that they would have the correct finish, and he took bag after bag of bolts and small parts to the shop for plating.

He worked even longer hours in his garage than usual. He found that Fred Farmer and his team from Pretty Cars had most often used exactly the correct and typical parts and methods of assembly, but he did spot items that needed to be changed—Brayden and his fellow judges had not noticed many of them. He simply shook his head when he realized that he could have been given even more deductions.

Roger scrutinized the judging sheets from the Rochester meet repeatedly with the greatest care. He all but memorized them. Every time he made a change to correct a part or condition that had resulted in a deduction, he checked it off and made a note of what he had done to correct it. When he had finished, he went over the deductions and corrections again, and then again.

The next NCRS event in his area was four weeks away in Nebraska. He now confidently looked forward to it. There was a car show in Sioux Falls the following weekend, and he thought he would enter the 1960 if Em'ly and Nell also wanted to exhibit there. When he called Em'ly, she told him to stop by her garage. "You simply must see what

Nell has done with the interior of your former Corvette."

Roger parked directly in front of Em'ly's open garage doors. As he had noticed on a previous visit, tools and car parts were strewn everywhere across the floor. Em'ly's copper car was again on jack stands with all four wheels removed, and Nell's yellow car had both seats sitting next to it. Roger smiled at the activity as he walked in.

"You should put up a sign that says 'Em'ly's Hot Rod Shop.'"

She grinned and said, "I'd like to do that, but I'm not sure this part of town is zoned for heavy industry."

The two of them sauntered across the garage to look at Nell's seats. They were bright, they were striking, and they were in good taste. Roger looked closely at the seams. "This is first-class work, Nell. Excellent! Brava! Brava!"

She smiled modestly at the compliments. "Thank you."

"I'd never have thought of such a bold design. You're an automotive artist as well as a master of your craft."

Nell silently beamed with pleasure.

"We should enter our cars in the Sioux Falls show next weekend."

"Yes, definitely, we want to show our cars in Sioux Falls," Em'ly said, "but we weren't sure that you were ready."

"I am."

"We can leave early Sunday morning."

"Dr. Strong," Nell said in a questioning tone, "can you do me a favor?"

"Of course."

"You have exhibited and judged modified Corvettes. On Saturday morning I'll have everything reassembled and cleaned on this car. Will you stop by and give me any final tips that might help at the show?"

"Sure. I'd be glad to do that. In exchange, will you ask your friend here to glance at my 1960 and tell me any last-minute changes that I should make?"

"Sure. I'll pester her until she provides all the advice you could possible want."

All three of them were smiling as Roger turned and left.

Very early on the cool, bright Saturday morning, Roger detailed his 1960 as well as he could—he wanted it to look its best when Em'ly inspected it. He then drove the Corvette over to her garage. As he pulled near, he saw that both Nell's 2004 and Em'ly's 1955 were parked in her driveway. The cars' complementary paint colors of millennium yellow and metallic copper glowed in the sunlight. He backed his car into a line with the two cars.

"Hey, is this the location of the car show?"

"Of course it is," Em'ly said with a welcoming smile.

"I have the new interior done," Nell said. "Tell me what you think of it."

Roger walked over to Nell's car, and he shook his head. "If I didn't know that this is the car that I had once owned, I would not have recognized it. The seats are perfect. I like the chrome-colored leather bolster surrounding the striped yellow leather insert. And the center console, shift boot, brake boot, and door handles echo the seat pattern—they're perfect. Nell, the seats and the whole interior are wonderful. My only suggestion would be to add yellow leather as an accent on the passenger-side grab handle."

"That's an excellent idea. It would be easy to do."

Roger looked rather humble. "When I had this car, every part of the interior was black. Boring Black was my theme. I suppose I thought that there was some reason it came from the factory that way—well, sure, the reason is that the Corvette designers lacked imagination, and I lacked it too. You certainly don't. Your interior work is so much better— you could call it a bright idea."

Nell said, "I worked pretty hard on that interior. I put to use a lot of things that I learned in my upholstery class."

"When you're showing a modified car, you're judged on the overall design and detail and the car's absolute cleanliness. I think the design and detail of the car are perfect, but naturally, I would think that. Perhaps you can see some additional changes that could make it better—you have a better color imagination than I have. The car looks clean today, but make sure to dust and polish it at the show before the judging. I used to even clean and polish inside the exhaust bezels."

Em'ly was examining Roger's 1960. After moving slowly around the car, she carefully examined the engine compartment. Roger gave Nell another round of praise for her car, and then he joined Em'ly. "So what do you spot that I could improve?"

"Remember that my research and study have focused on the 1955 standards, but I can give you some ideas about what to check. NCRS judges always look for the right paint on the engine in the right places. I notice that you don't have paint in several places on your engine—the distributor hold-down seems to be bare metal and there doesn't seem to be paint under the coil. Should there be Chevrolet Orange paint in those places? Similarly, there are places on your firewall that have parts mounted with black paint sprayed over the parts. I'm not sure what's correct for 1960."

"I'll check and get out my paint if necessary. Thank you."

"There's no hurry. The Sioux Falls show is not an NCRS event, but you'll want these things right before going to Nebraska."

Early Sunday morning, Nell drove her 2004 to Sioux Falls following two trucks pulling trailers. It was overcast, but rain was not predicted. At the show site, Nell and Roger had their cars side by side, and Nell was in the row directly in front of them. Because she had driven her car to the show, Nell had a good deal of work to do to make her car ready for judging. Roger helped her scrub bugs from the nose of the car with detail spray while Em'ly went in search of breakfast for them.

"You guys who trailer your cars sure have it easy," Nell said.

"It is a lot easier, but in my heart of hearts, I know it's sissy not to drive a Corvette to a show."

After eating very messy caramel rolls and drinking lukewarm coffee, the three plopped down in their chairs and watched the crowd of spectators flow by the cars. There was the expected admiration for the chromed engine on Nell's car, and, for the first time, the spectators were effusive with praise at the interior of the car. After noon, judges arrived. As Em'ly and Roger knew, they did not look for the same kinds of things that the NCRS judges focused on. It was obvious that they were simply stunned by the copper color of the 1955.

Nell returned to sit by her friends after judges had finished looking at her car. "They didn't seem to be impressed by anything about the car," she said. "They looked, they grunted, they made notes on their clipboards, and they moved on without saying anything to me."

Roger shrugged. "Perhaps they were simply keeping their thoughts and judgments to themselves."

"I suppose it's childish, but I really would like to win some kind of trophy. Do you think I have a chance?"

"I am sure that you have a very good chance to win an award, and you will win unless the judges are blind and stupid." He thought for a moment. "You are being very honest about your feelings. I share them—I want to win—and almost all exhibitors want to win. However, it's fashionable in this hobby to claim that you don't care."

As usual at a large car show, the awards were delayed well past the published time. When, at last, they were announced, Roger took second place in stock Corvettes, and Em'ly won first place. Both of them knew that at a non-NCRS show, the color of her car was a deciding factor. There were many modified Corvettes, and all three of them felt the tension as the trophies were announced. Nell won first place. She laughed and jumped from her chair and ran to accept the trophy. When she returned, she eagerly showed it to Em'ly and Roger.

One enormous trophy remained to be awarded. The Show Director took his time reading the name of the winner. "There were many, many great cars in this show, and all of them deserve a hand." There was perfunctory applause. "But there can be only one winner of this trophy. And the Best in Show is… Nell Underwood for her modified 2004 Corvette!"

Nell had been happy winning her division, but she was now paralyzed with glee. She laughed and cried with joy, and she sat grinning and wiped her cheeks in disbelief.

Em'ly laughed at her. "Girl, go get your trophy!"

When Nell returned, she held out the huge trophy in disbelief. Her friends stood looking at it and talking as most of the exhibitors packed up and left. "You two have given me a whole new world," Nell said with a look of honest gratitude. "I've done stupid, wrong things all my life, but now I have a new life with new interests and new friends. Thank you. Thank you. Thank you."

CHAPTER 26

Two days before the NCRS event in Omaha, Nebraska, Roger worked on his 1960. He was determined to do everything right. He had studied the judging sheets from the Rochester event, and he believed that he had addressed every area in which his car had suffered deductions. If a new part were needed, he had found one— an original from a salvage yard, if possible, or NOS parts—new old stock. He was amused by the oxymoronic term "new old stock," but he understood that it was supposed to mean original parts that had never been installed on a car, but could have been. Unfortunately, often what were advertised as NOS parts were parts manufactured long after the car was made, and they were only somewhat similar to original stock.

Sometimes a little paint or plating was needed to make the appearance of a cover or a bracket the color of the original. Roger sprayed Chevrolet Orange high-temperature paint on several parts of the engine. He was very careful that the paint went only where it was intended—he spent hours masking off parts that he did not want painted. He had boatloads of bolts, washers, and nuts plated silver cadmium, black phosphate, and gold cadmium, and he had sand blasted others and left them the natural metal finish. He installed them in the correct places, and he had a supply of bolts, washers, and nuts on hand for the future—all of them in bins organized and identified according to size and application.

He waxed the car with a carnauba paste wax and buffed it to achieve a bright shine, but it retained a rather low level of distinctness of image. The objects reflected in the paint were blobs that were blurred and fuzzy—it was precisely the appearance of the original DuPont Lucite acrylic lacquer paint. It looked exactly right—it looked typical.

Although the engine was clean, he went over it again. He polished everything in the interior and cleaned the windows. He vacuumed the trunk. He rolled under the car and rubbed a rag across the transmission to be sure it was free of dirt and the numbers could easily be read. He did the same thing with the drive shaft and rear differential. As he scrubbed the differential housing, he thought of its common name, the pumpkin, and he smiled at the appropriateness of the term based on its appearance. The rough edge of the rag caught on the housing, and tore. Obviously, he needed to remove the threads of cloth that clung to the differential. When he couldn't immediately reach some of them, he swore and threw a screwdriver the length of the garage.

Roger squirmed out from under the car and backed away from it and stood looking. He couldn't imagine what else he could do before the NCRS judges saw it. It appeared exactly like a brand new 1960 Corvette that was just off the showroom floor.

After he carefully locked the 1960 in his garage, he went to Em'ly's house to see if she was cleaning and polishing her 1955 in a similar manner. He was surprised when he was told that she and Nell were in the backyard next to the pool, and, sure enough, that's where he found them.

"I thought you would be cleaning and polishing your car," Roger said as he approached.

"Oh, that's been done for hours. Nell helped me, and we were finished in no time, and then we figured we would come out here by the pool and relax."

"We deserve it," Nell said with a smile.

They discussed the arrangements for travel to the event in Omaha. "Will Joey come along with us?"

"I hadn't thought to ask him. Do you want him to come with us?"

"Well, I always feel safer when you're both around."

"What about your brother Ben?"

"He's been acting strange lately. Maybe his business is going down the toilet, I don't know, but he sulks and crabs all the time, and he won't help me with anything. He certainly doesn't want to go with us to Omaha."

Roger took out his cell phone and made a call to the sheriff. "Hey, Joey. Would you enjoy an all-expenses-paid trip to Omaha tomorrow? … No, Em'ly says that Ben can't go with us. … I don't know—she says that he sulks and crabs and won't even try to help her. … Okay, I'll let you talk to her." It was agreed that they would start early, and Joey would drive Em'ly's truck and Nell would ride with Roger.

Their arrangements for the next day concluded, Roger relaxed in the mild sun and drank a margarita and chatted with the girls. Everyone was looking forward to the trip.

"In a way, I'm not surprised that Ben refuses to help me show the car," Em'ly said. "He never got along with Gordy. He made fun of the way Gordy dressed and how he talked about investments, and he even made jokes about his showing the Corvette, and he certainly didn't help Gordy with the car. Now he seems to have turned on me."

Roger didn't know how to comment on Em'ly's family situation, so he remained silent.

In the darkness of the early morning, two trucks pulling early Corvette show cars in trailers headed south on the interstate highway toward Nebraska. Roger's Hummer was in the lead. For a fall day, the weather was unseasonably warm. Storms, perhaps violent, were predicted. The clock on Roger's dash indicated that the sun should be rising, but the day remained dark. Lightning could be seen on the horizon ahead of the trucks. They apparently were driving directly into a storm, and it was not long before they were in it.

Nell tipped her head and listened to the *plung—mump—blung* of large raindrops hitting the top of the truck and the windshield. Roger turned on the wipers, and soon he had to increase their speed. Before long, the rain became a dense flood of water hitting the truck, and the wipers could not keep up.

"Do you think you should pull over and let the worst of the storm pass?" Nell was clearly concerned.

Roger turned on the hazard blinkers and pulled onto the paved shoulder of the road. In his mirrors, he could dimly see a pair of headlights behind him that indicated that Joey was also pulling off directly behind them.

As they sat waiting for the rain to let up, the sounds changed to *ping—wap—teep*. It was hailing. Hail stones the size of marbles hit the hood of the truck and rolled around as they were driven by gusts of wind. Then there was a *wap—bomp—crump*. The size of the hail was increasing. In the beams of the headlights they could see larger and larger white blurs falling and cracking into several pieces on the pavement. The sounds of hail hitting the truck grew louder as the ground became white.

The wind was fierce. Gusts made the heavy Hummer rock and made the hail strike with greater force. Water was driven through the side window seals and ran down the door panels in tiny rivulets. The rumble of thunder was continuous and lightning illuminated the sheets of blowing water.

Roger tried to reassure Nell. "This weather may look and sound bad, but it can't hurt us in this heavy truck, and the five or six thousand pounds of the loaded trailer will help keep us in place too."

After sitting silent, Nell spoke in a low voice. "When I'm in a bad place like this, I think of all the bad things that I've done—running with a gang, getting into trouble, going out with convicted felons, and I wonder if this is a judgment on me."

"I can tell you with certainty that it is not."

"How do you know?"

"In the first place, you've turned a new page, started a new life, and you would not now be suffering a judgment for distant past deeds."

"And in second place…?"

"I haven't done any of those things, and I'm in the same storm."

Nell laughed.

The hail suddenly stopped as if it had been turned off by a supernatural hand on a switch in the sky. The rain greatly diminished to a fine mist falling gently like the final rinse of a car wash. Roger put the truck in gear and slowly pulled back onto the highway. He peered in his mirrors to be sure that Joey was following. Some of the hail on the highway crunched under the weight of the truck, but it was amazing how quickly the hailstones melted, and soon they were simply driving on a wet road. A light rain continued to fall. Both trucks pulled off at the next gas station to get more fuel and to compare their thoughts on the storm.

The station attendant grinned at them and said, "Some weather! The radio said that the wind blew the roof off a hog barn just down that road."

They were soon back on the road, and the sky overhead cleared as they drove. Three hours later they pulled into the parking lot of their motel in Omaha. They checked in, and, a little later, they regrouped for supper at a steakhouse across the street from the motel. Soon they sat feeling stuffed and exhausted with their travel. They all were eager to get a good night's sleep, and agreed to meet early the next morning.

The NCRS event site in Omaha, like the Rochester site, had many volunteers who showed them where to park the trailers and pointed out the proper places for their Corvettes. Although this was a regional event, there were fewer cars entered than in Rochester. Roger wondered if the judging would proceed faster than it had in Rochester.

When the cars were dusted and ready for judging, a bright sun peeped out. Nell and Em'ly stood talking with the owner of another 1955 that was two cars away. Joey sat next to Roger behind his 1960. As Roger surveyed the other Corvettes that would be judged that day, the sheriff was lost in thought for a few moments. He confided in Roger. "I wanted to know if Ben would be on this trip because when we returned from Rochester, I asked to borrow his .38 revolver, and I sent it to the ballistics lab to see if it's the gun that killed Dean Tyler. If it is, I'll have to confront him. I'll get the test results next week. It would be rather awkward for me to be socializing with him at a car show one day and accusing him of murder the next day."

"Do you think that he killed Tyler?"

"Without any ballistic evidence, there's no reason to think so. I can't imagine a motive. For what it's worth, I was told recently that he badly needed the infusion of funds from Gordy's estate, but now Ben has frittered it all away, but, of course, that has nothing to do with Dean Tyler.

The first team of NCRS judges rounded the corner where T-shirts and hats were being sold. As they approached Roger's car, he could feel his stomach do a flip. Joey looked at the judges with an air of new respect—the kind of respect that he would normally give only to FBI agents.

"We're the Operations Team," the lead judge said. "Does everything work properly on your car?"

"I believe so. I checked and double checked."

"Good. We will not take long."

They worked very quickly. One judge stood in front of the car, and the other stood behind it as they asked Roger to pull on the parking lights, then the headlights, and dimmed them, then one blinker then the other, and then they wrote on their forms. The entire process took perhaps thirty seconds. They continued with every function on the dash and ended by asking Roger to move both seats all the way forward and backward. Because the large original steering wheel had been installed, Roger was rather squashed when he moved the seat forward. After only about fifteen minutes, the two judges compared notes and finished completing their scoring sheet.

The lead judge showed his sheet to Roger. "You said that everything works, and that appears to be true. There's only one deduction of 5 points because your tachometer is not zeroed out. It shows about 50 rpm when the engine's not running. You should be very proud of this car. Initial here."

As the day went on, the four additional judging teams inspected Roger's car. They did not work as quickly as the Operations team, and they seemed to find more deductions than the Operations guys—but not a lot more. By 2:00, all five teams had gone over his car. Roger sat with the notes that he had jotted down when the judges showed him the official judging sheets, and he was doing calculations.

"Em'ly, double check this for me. If my addition is correct, there are only 220 points in deductions, and 4500 minus 220 is 4280 and that is a little over 95 percent. Top Flight requires 94 percent. Is my math correct?

"Yes, it certainly seems accurate."

"Then I am the owner of a Top Flight Corvette!"

CHAPTER 27

Sheriff Bucket and Roger did a lot of conniving and told some white lies in order to assemble the people in one room who could be most directly connected with the deaths of Gordy Flowers, Dean William Tyler, and Dr. Rebecca Whelk. An important announcement would be made, the sheriff said, and a seminar room in Roger's building was the location of the event. It was directly down the hallway from the office in which Professor Whelk had died.

On a cold and dark early winter day with snow predicted, the group gathered. Nell Underwood, Em'ly Flowers, and Ben Flowers were the first to arrive, and they quietly took seats on one side of the large table. All three were informally dressed in jeans and sweaters. Darrell Yorick arrived late. He wore a business suit with his typical green shirt. Roger sat next to Joey. Several uniformed deputies stood unobtrusively in the back of the room.

The sheriff stood and cleared his throat and spoke. "I think we can begin. If you will all answer a few questions honestly, and if you are forthcoming, I think we can understand how three people died. Roger, I believe you have a question or two for Ben Flowers."

Roger stood. He felt rather foolish standing there impersonating a criminal prosecutor, but he would follow the role that Joey had requested. "Ben, do you know how many deans there are at this university?"

Ben looked very uneasy and confused—as if he were being asked a trick question. "One, I suppose. How would I know something like that?"

"That's fine. Do you know who was dean of Dr. Whelk's college?"

"Dr. Tyler was the dean at one time. Now, I don't know."

"I teach English literature," Roger said in a mild tone. "Do you know who my dean would be?"

"I told you I don't know who the dean is."

"If I taught business, would you know who my dean would be?"

"No!" I keep telling you, I don't know things like that." He was irritated.

"Thank you." Roger said politely and sat down.

The sheriff stood again. "Nell, on the morning that Professor Whelk died, where were you?"

"I was waiting for Dr. Strong in the hallway just outside his office."

"Did you see Dr. Whelk come up the stairs and walk toward her office?"

"Yes."

"Did you see anyone follow after her?"

"Yes…"

As Nell was about to continue—perhaps to say that she couldn't identify that person—Yorick interrupted her. "You can't believe anything that she says! She's just a tattooed delinquent, and she—"

Joey held his hand up as a stop sign to Yorick, and then he turned back to Nell and quietly smiled at her. "Who did you see?"

Nell was staring daggers at Yorick after he had called her names. "I saw a man follow Dr. Whelk toward her office. When Mr. Yorick gave me a loan at his bank, he asked me to keep quiet about seeing him there that morning."

"That's a lie." Yorick spoke without conviction.

"Mr. Yorick, what reason would she have to lie?"

"I don't know," he murmured.

"Mr. Yorick, several months ago, did you ask Dr. Whelk to have dinner with you?"

Yorick was surprised at the question. He hesitated and then said, "Yes, I did, but she turned me down. I came over here to ask her again, but—" He realized that he was telling more than he had intended.

"Were you about to say that you went to her office that morning to ask her out again?" When Yorick didn't answer, the sheriff prodded, "We know you were there."

"Okay. Yes, I was there." He paused and Joey was patient. Yorick continued, "Listen, I didn't do anything wrong!"

"Tell us what happened."

He looked down. "Well, you're right. I went to Rebecca's office that morning to ask her out—exactly what you thought. Her office door was standing open, and I saw her near the door with a folder in one hand and with her purse slung over her shoulder, and she was reading a half sheet, a note, that she held in her other hand. She glanced up at me, and as I started to talk to her about having a pleasant, innocent dinner with me, she looked down again and continued reading the note. I got a little angry that she was ignoring me, and I grabbed the note and pulled it out of her hand.

"She over-reacted—she acted as if I had assaulted her. She backed away from me and dug her hand in her purse. She pulled out a small gun and pointed it at me. Naturally, I was surprised that she carried a gun. I stepped toward her thinking that this was some kind of joke. I was shocked to see her lift the gun to her temple and shoot herself. She fell to the floor. I didn't know what to do. I knelt next to her and felt for a pulse, but there was none. I slowly stood up, and I felt frozen to the spot for a while. Then I backed out the door and hurried away.

"No doubt I should have stayed there and called the police. I wasn't thinking clearly. The only thing that ran through my mind was that I would be blamed for Rebecca's death if I was found on the spot. The sound of the gunshot still rang in my ears.

"I had taken only a few steps down the hall when I realized that I still had her note in my hand, but there was no way that I was going to return to her office and leave the note." He took a breath and quickly looked around the room.

"I knew that I hadn't done anything wrong, and so when I had the chance to ask Nell not to mention that I was in the building, I thought I should do that. I apologize for the strong words I just used about her."

The sheriff glanced at Nell who still looked angry and then back at Yorick. "Do you still have the note?"

"Yes. When I saw what it said, I thought I might need to produce it to prove my innocence in case something exactly like this happened."

"We will need that note. What did it say?"

"It was a suicide note. It said that she couldn't go on with everyone in the university working against her, and she would take some of them with her."

"Good grief!" Roger said. "Her plan was to attend the committee meeting and shoot some of the faculty—probably including me!—before taking her own life."

"That's what the note said."

"However," Joey added, "You interfered with her plan by showing up in her office and grabbing the note out of her hand, so she simply shot herself there and then."

"I guess so."

"We did some checking," the sheriff said. "The .22 found next to Dr. Whelk was the gun that shot the bullet that killed her, and it was the gun that she purchased a few months back in Connecticut. So far, Mr. Yorick, this all fits together with your account."

Yorick nodded in relief.

"But this isn't the end of the story. The ballistics lab also determined that Dr. Whelk's .22 was the gun that killed Gordy Flowers. Since she frequently wore a pink coat, and a woman wearing a pink coat was seen in the area the night that Gordy was shot, we believe that she killed him. Of course more investigation would be needed to prove a case against Dr. Whelk. Naturally, she can't be charged with anything now, but an important point to investigate concerns her motive— Dr. Whelk had no apparent reason to shoot Gordy Flowers. Why would she do that? Dr. Strong has a theory."

Roger stood up. "In Alfred Hitchcock's movie *Strangers on a Train,* two men who are complete strangers from completely different walks in life happen to meet while traveling on a train. Both men have someone in their life they wish were dead. They agree to each commit the murder that the other wants. In that way, even if suspicion were to fall on the killer, there would be absolutely no motive.

Sheriff Bucket continued, "Ben, were you an actor in a community production of 'Arsenic and Old Lace' with Rebecca Whelk?"

"So what?"

"Nell, did you do makeup for that play?"

"Yes."

"Did you ever see Dr. Whelk and Ben talking during rehearsals?"

"Yes—they were huddled together off in the back of the stage several times. I thought they were having some kind of affair, but then they quit meeting and didn't even talk to one another. I remember one day that the two of them passed through the green room, and they didn't even say hello."

"Em'ly, did you think that Dr. Whelk and your brother were having an affair?"

"No. On the contrary, I was surprised that Ben even knew her."

"Ben," the sheriff said, "we know that you badly needed money, and you wanted to inherit your brother's estate. You made a deal with Dr. Whelk just like in the movie. You asked her to commit your murder for you— you wanted her to kill Gordy—and she did exactly that."

Roger stood next to the sheriff. "In return, she asked you to kill her dean—she hated him because he had denied her tenure."

Joey said, "And you thought you had done exactly what she wanted. You purchased a .38 revolver in Texas, and you learned where the dean's office was, and you entered on a Sunday night and shot him. A witness, Dusty Rhodes, saw you there that evening, and the ballistics lab has determined that the bullet that killed Dean William Tyler came from your gun."

Roger said, "The only problem is that you shot the wrong dean! As you indicated when I asked you questions about deans, you don't know much about the administrative structure of a university, and when you found out that Tyler was a dean, you assumed that he was the man that Rebecca Whelk wanted dead, and you shot him."

Ben remained silent, but his look clearly said, *I screwed up*.

The two deputies moved toward Ben, and the sheriff read him his rights as he was handcuffed and lead away.

When Roger arrived home that evening, he found that a large important-looking envelope from the National Corvette Restorers Society had arrived in the mail. He sat at his desk, took a deep breath, and opened the envelope. The letter on the top of the packet of papers congratulated him for having earned a Top Flight Award for his 1960 Corvette. He examined all of the official judging sheets and other papers, and he looked up and grinned. Roger immediately phoned Joey to invite him to come to his garage to toast the Top Flight Corvette.

"I don't pretend to understand all that's involved," Joey said when he was settled on the old leather couch with a ceremonial beer in his hand. "However, I do know that NCRS Top Flight status is a big deal and you deserve praise for bringing this car up to that level."

"Thank you. I am proud of that turquoise Corvette. And you deserve praise for figuring out how those three deaths occurred."

"I would never have thought of the Hitchcock movie."

"You see—the arts are useful. Do you think Ben Flowers will be convicted?"

"I'm sure he will be. When he got to the station, he denied any guilt—he wanted to put all the blame on Whelk. He said that this was all her fault. However, in blaming her he also incriminated himself. He claims that she dreamed up the crimes and that he was simply caught in her conniving schemes. She told Ben that she hid in the bushes across from the airport because he had told her that Gordy would pass by as he went for his nightly jog. She shot and killed him, and then simply walked away. Later, she reminded him of his obligation to take care of her dean. As you thought, he had no idea that there was more than one dean. He walked across campus one Sunday night, and he had his .38 in his pocket. He was looking for an opportunity. He saw the sign on the business building that declared that the dean's office was in that building, and the light was on. He entered and shot Dean Tyler."

The two friends sat silent for a few moments drinking their cold beers.

"Now that you have achieved the highest honors with this Corvette, what will be your next challenge?"

Roger looked at his 1960 Top Flight Corvette and glanced toward a photo on his refrigerator of a T-bucket street rod that he had once entered in lots of car shows. "I've been thinking about building a loud, atrocious rat rod."